BLUES
AND
TROUBLE

BLUES
AND
TROUBLE

TWELVE STORIES

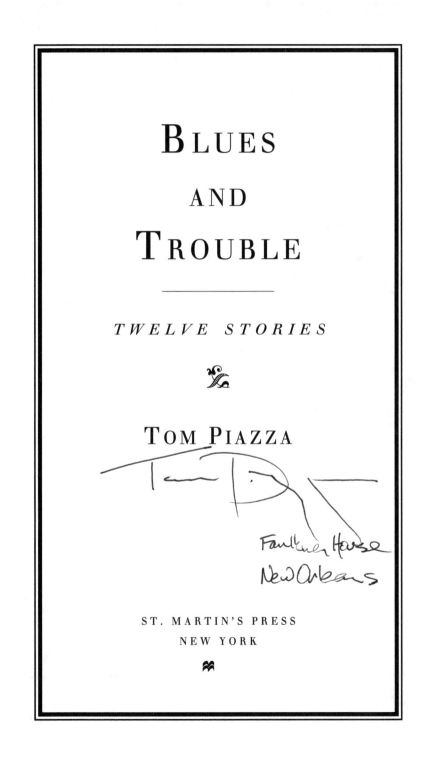

TOM PIAZZA

[signature]

Faulkner House
New Orleans

ST. MARTIN'S PRESS
NEW YORK

The stories in this collection are works of fiction. All of the events, characters, and institutions depicted in them are entirely fictitious.

"Brownsville" first appeared in *The Quarterly* (Vintage Books), "Born Yesterday" in *Story*, "Memphis" in *American Short Fiction*, and "C.S.A." in *The Double Dealer Redux*.

Library of Congress Cataloging-in-Publication Data

Piazza, Tom
    Blues and trouble : twelve stories / by Tom Piazza.
        p. cm.
    ISBN 0–312–13934–9
    1. United States—Social life and customs—20th century—Fiction.
I. Title.
PS3566.I23B58   1996
813'.54—dc20

                                                        95–39344
                                                        CIP

Design by Ellen R. Sasahara

First Edition: February 1996

10 9 8 7 6 5 4 3 2 1

ACKNOWLEDGMENTS

For various kindnesses, the author would like to thank Frank Conroy, James Alan McPherson, Norman Mailer, Stanley Crouch, Frances Kiernan, Cal Morgan, Gail Hochman, Marianne Merola, the Pirate's Alley Faulkner Society, and the MacDowell Colony.

The author is especially grateful to James Michener and the Copernicus Society of America for their generous support.

CONTENTS

FOREWORD

T he actual American story is always colder, hotter, and more mysterious than we would like it to be. But the reason we are always attracted to the serious tale of American life and place is endlessly at hand. Any impressive fiction with a United States pedigree subtly or muleheadedly opens discussion of the known and the unknown, reminding us of the heartbreak, the inspiration, and the moxie at the center of the way we in this country have shaped a life so completely modern it has made the rest of the world into a variety of mirrors. Even so, one part of our American blues is that we so often refuse to create the emotional technology necessary to fashion our own spiritual mirrors. Our preference is the distortion, usually the distorted sense we have of ourselves. We are on the run. We believe happiness is a matter of geography, or a matter of class, or of color, or that happiness hides its wiles inside a pile of money. Motion to *somewhere* is what we wish for. All along the run, the blues disturbs and reminds us, hiding like a pebble inside our favorite jogging shoes, or sitting just under our skin, a long splinter of emotional recognition denied. The blues never refuses to tell us whenever we are fugitives from the mirror.

Foreword

These are some of the things Tom Piazza is clarifying in *Blues and Trouble*. In his stories we read and hear a voice that has no fear of the dissonance between appearances and essences, the discordant harmony that results from so many out-of-tune lives. But these are neither self-righteous morality tales nor sneering attitudes disguised as stories; they are tales of our time and of our dilemmas. They have the empathy that gives them human momentum and pulls us into the deeps where we, too, must hold our breath and feel the pressure of the water. In various ways, the collection talks out of school about the fantasies underlying the poor workmanship that goes into the making of our American gods, who are usually human, past their prime, and so misunderstood we too frequently fail to realize that they were shoddy even at full power.

If those targets of worship are not human, they form some version of heaven on earth. That heaven on earth is the other side of the fence, the other side of town, in another state, or even a place left not too long ago. It is some slice of the world ungooed by the difficulties of where we are, someplace where loneliness has no dominion, where love is snug as a bug in a rug. Or the preferred fantasy is some immature idea of freedom, a kind of life never caught in the bear trap of decay, dissolution, and death; a kind of life in which we might strive to enslave someone else in a ritual of performance based on repeating forever or as often as possible the shadow plays of a golden time, when all was green and every dream seemed nearly palpable.

Huge splinters like that pass through the flesh of these stories, which are so American that they don't accept the contemporary rules of the game. These stories take place in the North and the South, the East and the West. The characters are black or white or both; are Mexican or Anglo; are Jewish or Christian. They are Americans, not solely the members of a single group the writer has been assigned to by virtue of an imposed and closed-off ethnic identity, a category at odds with both the challenges of democratic imagination in narrative and the precision necessary to achieve epic command of the varieties of the national voice. Tom Piazza's people don't belong to any particular class, but they are trying to make do within the heavily starched rituals and customs of the places where they find themselves. If not, they might snap the running legs of their spirits in the gopher holes of desperate nostalgia, in the demon cups of booze, in the never-never land clouds of marijuana, in the snorted-up lines of white powder laid out on a mirror that reveals no more to the whizzing onlooker than disembodiment. Whatever they are and whatever they do, the blues knows them well and is never shy about saying so.

That Tom Piazza is able to bring such different kinds of people and problems to the page while holding together the form of his book with the themes and the nuances of that deathless twelve-bar form on which so many variations have been played is something of a signal achievement in this period. Because Piazza knows the blues—the facts of having rambling on the brain, the facts of loss and longing, the resolutions of romance and the harsh, deceptive antidotes of anger—he is able to weave those conditions through his characters and give an overall structure to this volume that is willfully musical in its sense of variation. Try, for instance, "Responsibility" and "Burn Me Up," back to back, if you would understand my meaning. In that respect, Piazza is throwing his hat in the ring where *In Our Time* did its timeless tricks, or where *Go Down Moses* went for broke, each of those books a monument to the shaping of American tales for the gathered force of a novel. I am not trying to put the burden of competition with Hemingway and Faulkner on this writer; I am just laying out a way for this work to be understood as a whole. In their quick summoning, their mix of the concrete and the lyrical, all given orchestral balance by pitch-perfect dialogue, the first eleven tales achieve the literary success of a blues suite. The last, "Charley

Patton," is an evocation of the blues singer and the world that inspired his sound, the world that remakes that sound into flesh, blood, bone, machinery, cuisine, and shelter—the community that always sits on the edge of nature and carries the human part inside, where the percolating and the bursting of the bubbles within the heart detail the mysterious arrivals and collisions of passion. It is a worthy coda of twelve paragraphs that concludes a fine, fine mess of blues.

—STANLEY CROUCH

"We'll take the car and drive all night. We'll get drunk. We'll go fishing . . ."

—Dooley Wilson
to Humphrey Bogart,
Casablanca

BLUES
AND
TROUBLE

BROWNSVILLE

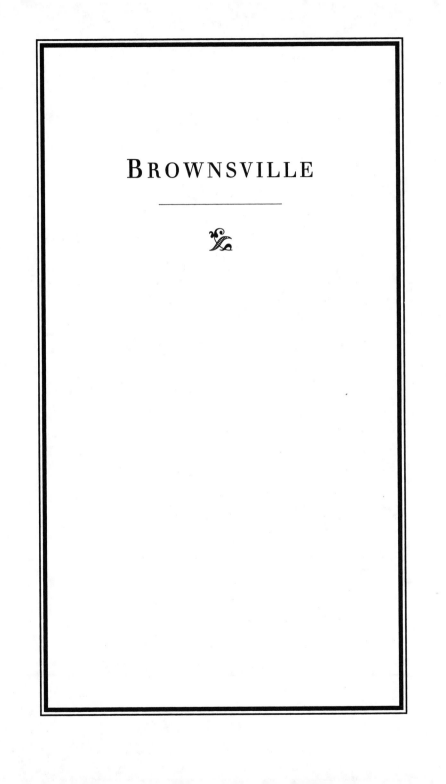

I've been trying to get to Brownsville, Texas, for weeks. Right now it's a hundred degrees in New Orleans and the gays are running down Chartres Street with no shirts on, trying to stay young. I'm not running anymore. When I get to Brownsville I'm going to sit down in the middle of the street, and that will be the end of the line.

Ten in the morning and they're playing a Schubert piano trio on the tape and the breeze is blowing in from the street and I'm sobbing into a napkin. "L.G.," she used to say, "you think I'm a mess? You're a mess, too, L.G." That was a consolation to her.

The walls in this café have been stained by patches of seeping water that will never dry, and the plaster has fallen away in swatches that look like silhouettes of countries nobody's ever heard of. Pictures of Napoleon are all over the place: Napoleon blowing it at Waterloo, Napoleon holding his dick on St. Helena, Napoleon sitting in some subtropical café thinking about the past, getting drunk, plotting revenge.

I picture Brownsville as a place under a merciless sun, where one-eyed dogs stand in the middle of dusty, empty streets staring at you and hot breeze blows inside your shirt and there's nowhere to go. It's always noon, and there are no explanations required. I'm going to Brownsville exactly because I've got no reason to go there. Anybody asks me why Brownsville—there's no fucking answer. That's why I'm going there.

Last night I slept with a woman who had hair down to her ankles and a shotgun in her bathtub and all the mirrors in her room rattled when she laughed. She was good to me; I'll never say a bad word about her. There's always a history, though; her daughter was sleeping on a blanket in the dining room. It would have been perfect except for that.

The past keeps rising up here; the water table is too high. All around the Quarter groups of tourists float like clumps of sewage. The black carriage drivers pull their fringed carts full of white people from nowhere up to the corner outside and tell them how Jean Lafitte and Andrew Jackson plotted things out, as if the driver knew them personally. The conventioneers sit under the carriage awning, looking around with the crazed, vacant stare of babies, shaded by history, then move on.

The sun is getting higher, the shadows are shortening, the moisture is steaming off the sidewalks. The Schubert, or Debussy, or whatever it is, has turned into an oboe rhapsody, with French horns and bassoons quacking and palmetto bugs crawling across the tile floor, making clicking sounds that I can't hear because the music is too loud. If she didn't love me, why didn't she just tell me so? I asked her why she lied to me and she said she was afraid to tell me the truth. In other words it was my fault. She doesn't even have a friend named Debbie.

I keep trying to look at what's right in front of me. I want to stop trying to mess with the past. The last thing she said to me was, "I have to get this other call." But I'm not going to think about her.

One cloth napkin.

One butter knife.

One fork.

One frosted glass containing partly melted ice and a slice of cucumber. Another frosted glass with similar contents. Where's the waiter? A small menu, marked with coffee along one edge. Breeze from a ceiling fan. Three Germans at the next table. The pictures of Napoleon must make them nervous. A waiter on a stool, leaning back against the wall by the ice chest, hair already pasted to his forehead with sweat.

A white Cadillac just backed into a car parked right outside, making a loud noise and partly caving in the wooden column supporting the balcony above the sidewalk. People are getting up and walking to the door, looking. The driver is black and is wearing a full Indian costume, plumes mushrooming as he gets out to look. He is about seventy years old; a five-year-old boy waits in the front seat. The driver gets back into the Cadillac and drives off.

———

One coffee mug at the next table. One crumpled pack of Winstons.

Hopeless.

I saw a sign once, on a building outside Albuquerque, that read ALL AMERICAN SELF-STORAGE. If you could just pay a fee somewhere and put yourself in a warehouse, just for a night.

Brownsville.

I picture a little booth at the edge of town, with a bored-looking woman sitting in it. You pay fifty cents and leave everything you can remember in a box with her. You walk down Main Street at high noon, wearing a leather vest, on the balls of your feet. The one-eyed dogs bark and shy away, walking sideways, eyeing you. You walk into the saloon, which is cool and dark, and order a bourbon. You look in the mirror behind the bar and talk to yourself in the second person. Maybe it would be better to stay outside in the sun.

Here is what morning is like in New Orleans. Just before the sky starts getting light, the last freight train inches its way through Ville Platte and the stars have drifted off to sleep. Slowly, the sky exhales its darkness and the trees look black against the deep blue over Gentilly. The houses along Felicity Street, and farther out toward Audubon Park, are cool to the touch, and dew covers the flower beds. A taxi pulls up to a traffic light, looks, goes through. The smell of buttered toast disappears around the corner and televisions are going in the kitchens of the black section. The St. Charles trolley, as unbelievable as it was yesterday, shuttles its first serious load toward the business district. Later, the men will have taken their jackets off and folded them in their laps, staring out the streetcar windows, caught in that dream. Already the first shoeshine boys are out hustling on Bourbon Street, and the first dixieland band is playing for the after-breakfast tourists, and the first conventioneers are climbing into carriages at Jackson Square, and the Vietnamese waitresses at the Cafe du Monde are getting off their all-night shifts, and luggage is lined up on the sidewalk outside the Hyatt.

If there was just some way to stay in it, to be there and see it without starting in. If there was just some way to wipe the slate clean. As soon as I can, I'm going to pay my tab and step outside. I'm closing my accounts and going to Brownsville. I'll leave everything at the edge of town. I'm going to walk in and take it from there.

BORN YESTERDAY

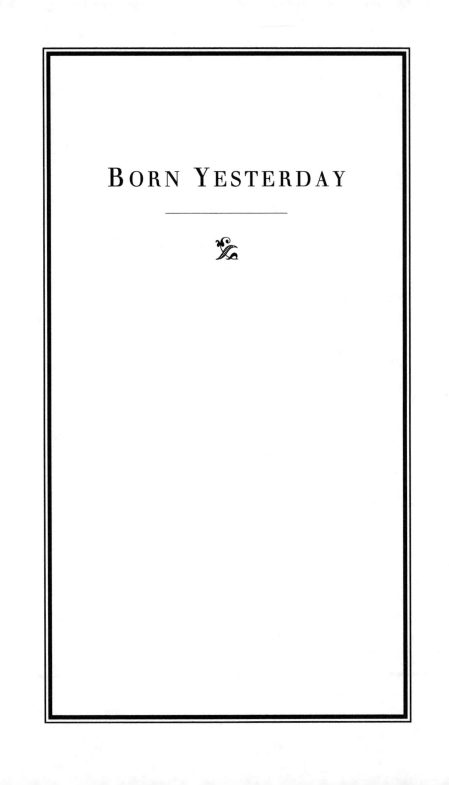

L aundromat in St. Augustine; I'm almost sure it's the same one I stopped in ten years ago on my way to Daytona Beach from the Smokies on spring break. It's raining now, too, stifling and damp. Fluorescent lights; endless hum of dryers. I'm not thinking about Louisa. At least the front door is propped open, so I can watch the cars steam by on Route 1 under the dripping trees. The rain can't last forever.

A little after dawn I pulled into a rest area at the Georgia border and shaved in a water fountain, and now my chin feels like it skidded on some gravel. There are two others in here: a fat woman wearing black stockings and washing a bedspread, and a good-looking housewife in her mid-thirties, with red hair and long legs leading up into a pair of red short shorts. I'm not in the market, though; not this morning. I just want to get to Daytona, go for a swim in the ocean and eat dinner at the Captain's Galley, if I can remember where it is. I don't want to have to make conversation.

I don't have that much stuff with me: a change of jeans, some underwear, and a couple of shirts is about it. And I've got no complaints at all with this Pontiac. What I paid for it doesn't matter, although it cost me $350. I bought it a week and a half ago in Waycross. It's sitting outside; feels like having a good woman waiting at home for you in bed. Or waiting in bed for you while you're in the kitchen cleaning up the drainboard. Although why she couldn't have cleaned the drainboard herself is another question, which you'll argue about later, for hours probably.

My clothes are dry, except the waistband and pockets of the jeans are a little damp. This is okay; I can hang them over the balcony railing at the motel. The housewife is stealing glances at me. She is almost beautiful, a little used-looking, with quick green eyes, red hair, and high cheekbones. I'm not biting, though; I don't want to get into it. I want to keep my mind quiet. You can only fold clothes so fast, but I do it as fast as I can and look forward to getting back to my car, still warm and waiting for me.

I get my stuff bagged up and throw it over my shoulder, smile and wave to her; she smiles a little exhaustedly, wiping her forehead with the back of her wrist. I turn away and try not to lunge for the door. Outside, I open the back door of the Pontiac, throw the bag in, slam the door shut, and climb in the front seat behind the wheel, dig out my keys. Daytona here I come.

Nothing happens when I turn the key in the ignition. Not even a shudder. I wait a second, try it again. Nothing.

The rain has slowed to an elegiac trickle; the sky is a few watts lighter, but still gray. "Come on, Mama," I say out loud, patting the dashboard soothingly. "Don't let me down." I turn the key again; no reply.

I try to think if I left the lights on, or the radio, except there's no radio. The guy said it gets funny sometimes when it's wet. I get out and open the hood, but I don't know what I expect to find. Car engines mean nothing to me. It's like looking at a map of Shanghai. I get behind the wheel again, leave the door open, turn the key one more time; no dice.

I get out of the car and look around as if I might see the answer printed on a tree somewhere. I can feel my dream of Daytona Beach dissolving before my eyes. I've been envisioning pulling into the motel parking lot, getting the key at the desk, going up to the room and changing into my bathing suit, running across the sand and slamming into the water, a hot shower and then dinner at the Captain's Galley. Now I face phone calls, tow trucks, explanations of the problem, and a long wait on a molded plastic chair next to a Coke machine, looking at racks of motor oil and fan belts, with a tinny radio going in the background. On Route 1, a blonde in a white halter top speeds by in a red convertible and disappears. In pure frustration I wind up and punch the back window on the driver's side, bellowing the word "whore" as thousands of tiny fissures materialize in the glass.

I feel better for about half a second until I see all the blood on my hand, and now I realize that on top of spending hours in a gas station, I'll probably get to hang out in an emergency room somewhere waiting for stitches, and fill out a whole medical history besides. I'm trying to think of something even more destructive that I can do, that won't bounce back and hit me in the face, dripping blood on the asphalt, as the housewife walks out the front door of the laundromat. She looks at me, smiling quizzically for a second, until she notices my hand.

"My God," she says, setting down her laundry basket. "Are you all right? What happened?" She comes over, looking at me searchingly.

If I could say something in Ukrainian, or Hindi, or start babbling pure nonsense syllables, I would, but the look of concern on her face is so genuine, and I say, "The car wouldn't start."

She looks at me blankly and I realize that this isn't really an explanation, so I say, "I got mad."

Now her expression is slightly darker, maybe a hint of fear in there somewhere. I don't want to scare her, so I say, "It was the culmination of a lot of small frustrations," and try to smile sheepishly.

She gives up trying to understand what I'm saying and looks at my hand. I'm a little dizzy, and I lean up against the Pontiac, feeling a pang of sadness that I punched it. She turns, says, "Wait a second," walks over to her laundry basket, pulls a T-shirt off the top and comes back over.

"Here," she says, taking my wrist.

"Wait a second," I say. "Don't ruin the shirt."

She ignores me and gently wipes the blood from the back

of my hand, looking at it, red hair falling around her face. "It's not too bad," she says. "I don't think you need stitches." I'm trying to breathe deeply from my stomach so I don't pass out. She's turning my hand slightly as she examines it, and I can see her breasts inside the shirt, and I'm getting turned on even though I know it'll only mean trouble. "You should get it dressed," she says.

She looks up at me. Her eyes are interested but cautious; she could size you up quickly, but she's got a real vulnerable side. Definitely not born yesterday, I think, but youthful anyway.

"Do you know where there's a hospital around here?" I say.

"Sure; there's Sister of Mercy on Rehoboth Avenue. But I can fix it up for you if you'd like. The ER there is a trip. You'll be waiting around all day."

It's hardly a choice. I get into her car. I'm nervous; this is a major detour. But between a couple hours in the ER and a ride with her . . . She loads her basket into the back, grabs my stuff out of the Pontiac, starts up the car, and we pull out.

I'm sitting in the passenger seat of her Chevy, hissing down Route 1 under the dripping trees. The rain has stopped.

"I've got first-aid stuff back at my house," she says. A couple of seconds go by. "You look pretty tired."

It feels so good to hear this note of compassion—plain, sweet, generic feminine compassion—that I close my eyes and put my head back on the seat, and I'm about to tell her my whole story, but I yank myself back in time. I just say, "Yeah. I am pretty tired." Not wanting to be rude, I add, "I drove all night."

She doesn't say anything, just takes the right fork at a blinking light, and we're driving past a strip of delis, dress shops, a newsstand, a diner. I'm in the aftermath of the adrenaline rush, crashing. I can feel the warmth around my ears. The car smells vaguely of gasoline. The hand hurts some; I've got the T-shirt wrapped around it. I feel like I should say something, but I don't know what to say: "Do you live around here?" "Can you believe this rain?" "Why don't they put another teller in at this branch?" I'd rather jump off the roof than start with that shit. So I just sit; this was her idea anyway.

We make a right on Judith Lane, a plain suburban street with spindly trees, tiny plots of land, crumbling sidewalks. I'm breathing from my stomach. She pulls into the driveway of a white split-level house with black shutters and cuts the engine. We get out; I move to help her with the laundry basket, but she shushes me away, saying to take care of my hand. I fully expect the worst as we approach the door, except I'm not sure what the worst is, short of an avocado-colored refrigerator, a cute red-haired son about ten years old who looks up at me suspiciously and doesn't respond to my questions, and newspaper clippings attached to the refrigerator door with little magnets. My impulse is to run screaming down the street, leave the car at the Speed Wash and take a cab to Daytona Beach; it couldn't cost much more than $150. She gets the front door open and we walk inside.

We are in a small entryway, with a stair going straight down on the left and one going up on the right. At eye level on the right is the carpeted floor of the living room; down at the bottom of the stairs on the left I can see wood paneling. So far nothing bad has happened. She whistles an "I'm home" whistle, and I think, Here it comes. Hubby coming up the stairs in a cardigan sweater, or no hubby, just little Johnny, or maybe neither, but a guy with a bandanna around his head and a black Harley-Davidson T-shirt, who paints pictures of Jesus in the oil-burner room, has a mustache, fat. . . . But none of them comes, only a gray tiger kitten who peers down at me from the ledge made by the living room floor. The cat has one brown eye and one green eye. I scratch its ear and say, "Hi."

"She has six toes, too," she says, and I realize I still don't know her name. She disappears down the stairs with the laundry basket and yells up, "Go ahead upstairs; I'll be right up. There's soda in the fridge, or whatever."

Laminated wood-grain cabinets, swag lamp over the kitchen table. No signs of family life—no pictures or clippings on the refrigerator. A bay window looking out on a backyard with a clothesline. I'm sweating horribly. All I want is some peace and quiet, lie in the sun, Captain's Galley, booth in the corner, no questions, please, God . . .

"How are you feeling?" she says, walking into the kitchen.

"Why don't you sit down and I'll take care of your hand."

I pull out a chair from the kitchen table and do as I'm told. She unwraps the T-shirt from around my hand, and the air smarts.

"Sting?" she says.

"Yeah," I answer, tersely. Relax, I tell myself. What's happening is what's happening. She's unscrewing the cap from a bottle of alcohol, and the bracing, medicinal smell is suddenly a dominant theme of the moment. She applies it with a cotton swab and it burns. I find this cleansing—pure sensation, and a great relief. As I'm savoring this sweet relief, she says, "What's your name?"

I feel as if a noose has just tightened around my neck with a sickening yank.

"Frank," I say immediately. This is a lie, but what does she have to know my name for?

"I'm Christine," she says, opening another bottle. "This is going to sting some." She swabs some of the peroxide onto the abrasion. The back of my hand looks like a side of souvlaki. The peroxide bubbles like grease spreading over a griddle, and I breathe in sharply.

"Are you from Georgia?" she says, trying to make conversation to take my mind off the pain. She noticed the plates on the car.

"No," I say, truthfully. As I sit there watching the fizzing die down on the back of my hand, I realize I can't keep giving one-syllable answers all night; she's being too nice. So I say, "I hitched out from California," and feel myself going into a controlled skid.

"You're from California," she says, smiling rhapsodically. "What part?"

"Hollywood," I say. I'm in too deep now to go back; I've never been west of Ohio.

"I've always wanted to go there," she says. "What's it like?" She's dabbing some of the excess peroxide off my hand and I can't watch anymore.

"About what you'd expect," I say. "Weather's great. Palm trees. Ocean."

She looks up at me for a second, then looks back down at my hand, and I wonder if she knows that I'm lying, so I scrabble around for a few more things to say to make it sound more real. "I was trying to act," I say. "I couldn't get any parts."

"TV or movies?" she says.

"Movies, mainly." It's an oddly sophisticated question to ask, it seems to me. "Did you ever do any acting?" I say.

"Me? No," she says, unrolling some gauze. "Never did."

"You could," I say. "You're sure pretty enough." She kind of smiles without looking up at me. She's wrapping the gauze around my hand, and it feels warm and dry.

She finishes taping it, then she reaches over to the drainboard for a pack of cigarettes. After she lights one she shakes some hair out of her face with a flick of her head and blows some smoke out into the air. We just sort of sit there for a minute with nothing to say. I wish I had some ideas but I don't. I feel as if I've escaped from a chain gang, and all I can think about is getting back on the run again.

As if she was reading my mind, she says, "You can leave

if you want to. I'll drive—" Then she gasps as she looks at my shirt, which has blood all over the side of it. "Oh, God," she says.

"Where did that come from?" I say, pulling it around to look at it.

She leans over and gingerly lifts the shirt; it seems that the blood just came off of my hand, unnoticed by us; no gash or anything on my ribs.

"Take it off," she says. "I'll . . . let me see; the guy who I sublet this place from left a bunch of clothes upstairs. We can wash this out real quick. Hang on." She hops up and leaves the kitchen.

Now I'm looking out the kitchen window, across the backyard, at a split-rail fence. The sun's coming out. There's always a plot somewhere to get you itching and start the meter running. I don't want a plot. I just want to eat some grilled sole at the Galley and not think about any-thing. I want to feel the cold water on my face and cross the river on the bridge near the place where the good trout held themselves in the current when we came back from the war.

She comes back into the room with a shirt in her hand. "This isn't great, but at least it's not soaked in blood," she says. It's pale green, with a vague paisley print in it. It looks like it was made from her grandfather's undershorts. I'm trying not to show my distaste, which is ludicrous, since I've been wearing this Tipitina's T-shirt for three days. I take it off, put it in the sink, put on the new one and button it up. Then suddenly I'm just really depressed. It rolls over me. My hand is busted up, I'm wearing somebody else's shirt,

I'm running around Florida using a fake name, my car is dead. This woman is being so nice to me, and it's like I'm not here at all.

"Are you all right?" she says.

"Sure," I say. "I'm fine." I'm crying.

"Hey," she says. "Hey," and I feel her arms around me. "It's okay. Wow; I knew something was wrong." She's petting my head, and I just lay my head on her shoulder and cry. I can't tell you how much I need this.

After a minute or two I put my hand around the back of her neck and kiss her. She kisses back as if it's what she had in mind the whole time. She kisses hungrily, like she's been imagining having someone to kiss. I try to slow her down a little by tugging on her hair in the back.

She stands up and pulls me by the hand, and I follow her out of the kitchen and upstairs.

It's about an hour later. She has dozed off and I'm lying on my back, staring up at the ceiling.

Louisa.

Why do I see her dresser with the chipped white paint and the tattered lace runner as if I were standing in her room? Why do I see her red plaid vest hanging on her closet doorknob? I can feel the cold air, with all the stars out, when I was shoveling the snow away from her car. I can feel how warm she felt in a flannel nightgown when I'd wake up in the middle of the night.

The dogs are baying in the distance. These peach-colored

walls and new-smelling carpeting mean nothing to me. I'll never escape.

She stirs a little, turns her head toward me on the pillow, opens her eyes. "Hi," she says.

"Hi," I say back.

She frowns a little and says, "Is anything wrong?"

"Nothing's wrong," I say, stretching nervously.

"You want to leave," she says.

"No," I say. "I'm a little worried about the car, I guess." It's lame, but it's the best I can do.

She lies there with her eyes shut and a few strands of red hair across her nose and upper lip. She really is beautiful, or pretty. Something warm about her. But I can't stay put right now.

"Let me know when you want to go," she says.

She's not making a fuss or laying any kind of trip on me, which makes me like her even more. Maybe in a few days, if I stay in Daytona that long, we can get together and have a good time. I could explain things to her then, and we could hang out.

I get up and go to the bathroom. When I get back to the bedroom I scrunch down under the sheet on one elbow, next to her. "Hey," I say. "I don't want to, but I should probably get going."

She drives me back to the Speed Wash. It has stopped raining and has turned into a beautiful afternoon, perfect for a drive, except that I'll probably spend it in a garage someplace. She gave me her phone number on a folded piece of paper that I've got in the breast pocket of the shirt, which she's giving me, but she's basically acting like she never wants to see me again. I don't blame her, but I don't know what else I can do. I should probably ask her if she wants to have dinner, but I can't deal with it. The project has been to get to Daytona, and I can't change it. I'm locked into it.

We pull into the parking lot; the Pontiac's still there, with its shattered window. The sun is glinting off the rear bumper. "I guess I'll give it one more try," I say, "before I call the tow place." She says she'll wait while I give it a try.

I get in and turn the key; it shudders, lurches. Then it dies. It seems to want to run, though. I start her one more time and it turns over and grumbles to life. It's gurgling but running. I can't believe it. "It must have been wet before," I yell out the window to Christine, over the revving engine. I'll have to get the starter looked at, and take care of the window, but I can do all that in Daytona. Christine is in her car, with the window down, watching me.

I climb out of the Pontiac, leaving it charging. "Look," I say, bending down and talking to her through the car window. "Thanks for taking care of me." She's looking up at me inscrutably, like she just can't figure me out. "After I get myself a little rested up, I'll call, if you think you'll still like to get together."

"Whatever," she says, putting the car into reverse. "Good luck." She backs the car up and I hop away as she wheels around, pulls out of the parking lot and heads back down Route 1. I watch the car until it disappears. I can call her from Daytona in a day or two, after I cool out.

I get into my good old Pontiac, pat the dashboard and say,

"Stay cool, Mama," slide her into gear and ease out of the parking lot. Daytona here I come.

I'm in the Captain's Galley, about halfway through my sole. It looks pretty much the way I remember it—lobster pots and nets strung up on the plank walls, gray-painted picnic tables. I'm sunk down into one of the booths by the windows, wearing my shades and glancing through the paper, which I'm having trouble concentrating on. They put too much paprika on the fish. I want to know why a woman insists on borrowing books that you both know she'll never read.

I wish I weren't feeling this way. If the Pontiac had started when I finished my laundry and I had been able to come straight down here, everything would have been fine. But now I'm just killing time. For that matter, why should it be so hard to just call the movers and move the couch back to your brother's house? Why does it take a month and then I have to do it after all?

After a while, I get the check and leave.

Outside, the palm trees loll overhead against the orange sky, and the one-story stucco buildings stare into the lurid sunset. I start down Fairview Avenue toward the ocean. The main question is what I'm going to do tonight to keep from losing it. The way I feel right now I might just bag it and get drunk and go to sleep. There was a place when I was down here ten years ago, called the Pink Lady, or the Pink Pussycat. It was on Ocean Avenue, I think. I had seen it when we hit town, on our way to the hotel, with a sign out front saying JAM SESSION—5 TO 9 P.M. I drove down there late in the afternoon, around five-thirty. It was dark as a cave inside, filled with hookers. The electric bass player was the leader; he had a big felt cap and shades, and across the front of the bass were stick-on letters saying BASIE. Maybe I'll just drive all night to Key West. A couple is leaning against a white convertible, making out. The girl is short, with red hair, sunglasses up on top of her head, and she's wearing a short denim skirt. His hands are all over her ass.

I can't stand it anymore. I cross the street to the parking lot of the Coral Arms, a turquoise motel, and head for the office.

It's a small office; a guy's watching TV behind the desk. He's wearing metal-rimmed, math-club glasses and a tie with a knot as big as a fist at his throat.

"I'd like to use a phone," I say. He gestures behind me without taking his eyes off the TV.

It's not the ideal setting. The phone is sitting on a low table, ten feet from the desk, next to a copy of *Sports Afield*. On the wall above the table is a clock with a metal starburst effect around it that looks like it would kill you if it fell on you. I don't have much of a choice.

I feel like a junkie picking up a spike. The familiarity of the heft of the receiver, the acceleration of knowing relief is on the way. I push O, the Massachusetts area code and number, and the operator comes on and I say, "Collect from Luke." My heart is pounding so hard I can hardly get the words out in a calm voice.

The operator says, "Your name again, sir; I'm sorry I can't understand you."

"*Luke,*" I say. "Can you understand that? Luke, as in the Bible. Luke."

"Collect from Luke. One moment; I'm ringing."

The moment feels as if it's spread across an eternity, like taking off at the end of a ski jump, or skydiving before the chute opens out, or maybe the moment between when they kick the chair out from under you and the rope tightens around your neck with a sickening . . .

"Hello."

"I have a collect call for anyone from Luke; will you accept it?"

There's a long moment's pause, and she says, "Yeah." The operator clicks off and she says, "Hi. What's up?" Breezily, as if I'm a neighbor just calling for an afternoon chat and interrupting her in the middle of paying bills. "Where are you?"

"Daytona Beach," I say.

She laughs as if I had told her I just enrolled in a baking course. "What are you doing down there?" She's eating something.

"I just had dinner at the Captain's Galley," I say. "I was down here ten years ago after that time in the Smokies that I told you about, on spring break."

"With . . . Gus. Right?" She's stoned. "The guy from Ohio."

"Gusto," I say. "Right. Anyhow . . . I'm out by the beach, and . . . I don't know. Why don't you come down here?"

"Oh . . . *God* . . ." she hollers, holding the phone away from her mouth; I can hear her voice echoing, which means she's sitting in the living room. Then, with her voice right back in my ear, she says, "You're crazier than I am. You weirdo."

"What are you eating?" I say.

She laughs her sheepish, bad-girl-caught-in-the-act laugh. "Milky Way."

This is it—the familiar driver's seat. The month and a half since I've seen her has melted away like nothing.

"Maybe I should come up," I say.

"When?"

"I don't know. I'd come up tonight."

"You would, too."

I could just leave the car at the airport. If things went wrong again, I could just fly back down and pick up where I left off. Even as I'm thinking this, a voice is telling me I'm making a gigantic mistake. I tell the voice to take the night off.

"You want to see me, huh?" she says.

"Let's get together," I say. My heart is beating so hard I have to consciously breathe from my stomach.

"But didn't we say this was what we can't do?" she says.

"Well, then . . . it was just something we said. We've said all kinds of things. If you want to see me, and I want to see you, that's . . . it. That's what matters now. Right?"

"But I don't know if I can see you right now," she says. "We said we had to take some time off."

"But just because we said that's what we were going to

do doesn't mean we have to do it," I say. This is an important point. "Who says things have to stay the same? Maybe we could get together and figure out some way—"

"I can't do this anymore," she says, breaking in. She's crying now. Somehow I've said something wrong, played it wrong. "I can't see you right now," she says. "It's fucking with my head. I can't do it anymore."

I have this bad feeling in my stomach that she's been thinking about this a lot, and starting to think in a pattern and there's no one around to give her the other side. The main thing is to make her realize that I understand.

"It's open," I hear her holler, her mouth away from the phone. There's a pause, then she says, "I'm on the phone; I'll be off in a minute." An indistinct voice in the background says something and she laughs.

Suddenly I'm aware of the sound of the television coming from the hotel desk ten feet away.

"Hey," I say, into the receiver.

"Sorry," she says.

"You going out?"

"Yeah."

"Who are you going out with?"

"Stop. It's just a friend."

"What if I come up?" I say.

"I can't pick you up . . . I can't go to the airport. It's been a long week; I can't do it."

"Hey," I say, "I'm willing to fly there from Florida and you can't even pick me up?"

"Don't *yell* at me."

There is a crucial point here that I'm not getting across to her.

"I'm not yelling," I say. "Why can't you pick me up?"

There's a pause. She's covering her mouthpiece.

"I have to get off the phone."

"What are you talking about?" I say.

"I just can't talk to you right now. It's not your fault. I'm sorry."

She hangs up.

I'm standing in a small room. I'm holding the receiver. Wait a second.

The television is going.

This is not going to go down this way.

I punch in the numbers again, jab, jab, jab. There is no way this is going to go down like this.

Ring.

There are a few more things I have in mind to say. I haven't been running around all over the place like a maniac just to be hung up on. If she's going to cross off a year out of both our lives, fine, but she's going to hear a couple of things first.

Ring.

I can see the living room, with its bare floor, and the couch she borrowed from her brother and still hasn't returned. I can see out her window to the basketball court across the street, and the steeple with the clock in the distance. Her car is downstairs, parked at the curb, with the beach chairs still in the trunk from last summer. She still has those art books I picked up at the auction on Plum Island.

Ring.

Answer the fucking phone. She has gone down the hall to see whoever has come to take her out. They are probably in the kitchen. All the pictures of me have doubtless been taken off the refrigerator. I'm sure she's put up pictures of her drunk friends from the state university instead, and postcards from Debbie telling her about getting laid in a Jacuzzi in Aspen. The front right burner on the stove still has the blue enamel burned onto it from the bottom of the tea pot she left sitting there for a half hour with no water in it. Answer the phone.

Ring.

We did it in every room of that apartment. We did it on the stairs. I remember the way she looked the first night we went out and ate Mexican food, back in the summertime, with her treacherous blue eyes and red hair. We drove out across the marsh to Plum Island, with the yellow moon hanging low over the ocean. At Christmas she went down to New York and left all her presents in the trunk of her car overnight. They got stolen and she didn't know it until she got to Kingston. I had a 103-degree fever and she had come to visit anyway. She gave me a blanket; that was the one thing they hadn't stolen. She bought it up in Kittery.

Ring.

If she thinks I'm going to give up, she's wrong; I'll hang on this phone until the ringing drives her crazy. What about that night when we sat on the driftwood log out on the beach and pushed each other off and lay in the sand laughing like idiots? What about when we had Italian food in the North

End and stayed over in the Howard Johnson's? Where are you now, why am I in Florida, why am I running like this, why can't you hear me, why don't you listen . . .

I take the receiver and grab it by the mouthpiece and wind up and whack it as hard as I can against the phone, whack it again, slam it down, can you hear this? are you listening to this? whack, and a piece of the plastic cracks off and shoots across the room, slam again, "Hey," the guy behind the desk says, but he's no part of this, then I pick up the whole phone and slam it against the wall, making a big rent in the yellow wallpaper; the receiver has an irregularly shaped piece cracked out of it, like out of a doll's head, and the guy is coming around the desk, and inside the receiver I can see the red and green wires, and it's over. I can feel it's over. This is the way these things end. I'm standing here. I just let the phone drop.

"What the fuck . . ." he's saying with his giant tie and math-club glasses, coming toward me.

"Hold it," I say, pointing my finger at him like Sidney Poitier in *In the Heat of the Night*. "Relax." I pull out my wallet and drop a twenty on the table. "Buy a phone."

"Hey," he says as I walk toward the door.

"Fuck you," I say over my shoulder. I push open the screen door and step outside into the scented evening air and start across the parking lot.

The heat is coming off the asphalt. The Mustangs and Thunderbirds are parked along the curb. The birds are flying way up in the orange streaks of the sunset. I walk toward the water. Everybody's going someplace. The cars are growling at stoplights, itching to get going.

I cross Ocean Avenue and walk through the parking lot of one of the hotels, the Phoenix, out to the sand, walk until I stop and look up and down the beach in either direction.

Somebody has brought their car out onto the beach, maybe half a mile down. Small breakers detonate on the sand, then hiss as they recede. Way in the distance tiny lights twinkle, probably hotels. I keep walking, and when I get to the water's edge I keep walking, and when I'm in up to my knees I take two steps and dive in headfirst. I stay under for a few seconds, with my shirt and jeans dragging and clinging in the water, then I break up through the surface, stand up and squeeze the water off my face with the palms of my hands. The gauze on my right hand is soaked and scratchy against my face.

The sky is getting dark. Up and down the beach contrasts are flattening out; everything is in tones of blue and gray, with the beading, glinting lights coming on now all along the shore. The water is streaming down my chest under my shirt, and wobbling up against my belly and the small of my back. Later I'll think about what I'm going to do tonight. But for now I'm just standing here, in up to my waist, looking around, and I realize that, for the first time all day, I'm not trying to get somewhere else.

C.S.A.

S quire Jack's Antiques and Memorabilia is located in the shell of an old Chevrolet dealership between Madison and Union Avenues, out by Danny Thomas Boulevard in downtown Memphis. The area was deserted by the middle class after Martin Luther King's assassination in 1968, and it has been empty feeling and desolate ever since. The few historic sites that escaped destruction during urban renewal—a Victorian mansion, a famous recording studio—are now nursed like fragile sprouts in the hopes that a tourist industry will grow up around them. Throughout the city, people draw a precarious sustenance from what is left of the past, like shipwreck survivors clinging to pieces of a smashed hull.

A rusty glow bathed the sides of the buildings out along Union, and the lowering sun filtered through the haze off the Mississippi and the dust rising off the fields around West Memphis, across the river. Delmar, a black man in late middle age, was sweeping up in the front of the store, moving between the cases full of old iron trains, tin boxes, cast-iron figurines and other artifacts, rocking, as he moved, with a limp from a childhood case of polio. He wore a St. Louis Cardinals cap pulled down low over his thick-framed glasses, and an unlit half-cigar was appended to his mouth. The Squire, a tall white man with white hair and a pink face, was taking care of a customer in the back of the store, a thin, hawk-faced man with piercing gray eyes. The Squire looked at the top of the thin man's cap as he peered down into the case at a cigarette lighter with an enameled swastika set into it.

"How's Mrs. Lewis doing out there?" the Squire said.

"She's all right, thank you," the thin man said. "I'll tell her you asked for her."

"I know she was interested, I don't remember if it was for her husband or her brother, in disposing of some materials. This was a few months back. Do you remember that?"

"I believe she gave up for a while," the customer said, still peering into the case. "She had trouble finding someone to handle it."

"I was full up at the time myself. And you have to be so careful with Nazi and C.S. stuff."

The thin man took a step to the left; he was looking at a large red Nazi flag. After a moment, the Squire pulled it from the case and spread it out on the glass.

"Now, what would something like that be worth to you? It's seen better days." He smoothed down the corner. There was some fraying along the sides.

"When is that from?"

"That would go back to around 1948," the Squire said. As he put it away, he said, "Tell—was his name Henry?— tell him I've got a good assortment in the back, some gorgets and all in good condition, too. I don't have room for it all in the cases."

The jingle bells on the glass front door rang, and the Squire looked up to see a young couple walk in. The man wore a pink alligator shirt and a pair of plaid Bermuda shorts, and the woman who accompanied him wore a white halter top snugly over her small breasts and a pair of candy-striped shorts, with sunglasses up in her curly black hair. They were obviously Yankees, he thought, unless they were Jews from Louisville or someplace.

Delmar leaned the broom against the wall and spoke to the young couple, saying, "If I can help you with anything, let me know." He pulled up the brim of his Cardinals cap and wiped his oily forehead with a kerchief, then set the cap back properly.

"Thanks," the young man said. "We'll just browse a little if that's okay."

"That's fine," the black said, adjusting his cigar between his teeth and rocking, limping, around behind the front counter by the register.

They were Northerners, indeed, from Boston. They were in Memphis for three days before heading to St. Louis to see a cousin of hers. The woman, whose name was Sheila, hadn't wanted to come to Memphis. She hadn't wanted to come south at all. Her parents were Jewish activists who had worked peripherally in the civil rights movement; her older sister had gone to Cuba to work with the Venceremos Brigade in the sixties. Since childhood she had pictured the South as a distant, evil kingdom.

Jeffrey, her husband, was a blues fan, and had always wanted to see Memphis, which called itself the capital of the blues. As his due for spending three days with her cousins, she agreed to spend three days in Memphis. They had passed their first afternoon in the city strolling up and down legendary Beale Street, once a teeming center for black entertainers, now a two-block historic district where pizzerias and souvenir stores occupied the carefully preserved husks of pawn shops and honky-tonks. It was as empty of people as an amusement park in November. They had spent the earlier part of this next day trying to locate some center of gravity in the city, but it was eluding them. She hadn't hid her impatience, although she had softened a bit as she felt his disappointment deepen.

The hawk-faced man was gone; in the back, the Squire finished tidying up, closed and locked the case, and walked up front. "How y'all today?" The thin man made him nervous; he was glad he had left.

"We're doin' just fine," Jeffrey said, in the light Southern accent he had picked up in the day and a half they had been down there.

"Lookin' for anything in particular?"

Sheila shook her head, looking down in the case, and Jeffrey said, "Do you have any old records?"

The Squire said, "No, they're too much trouble to handle. I'll tell you what, you might want to try the flea market they have at the drive-in out on North Parkway if you're gonna be around tomorrow." He gave them directions.

Dust hung in the air as the afternoon sun came in the front window. Delmar sat on a stool, not talking, looking out to the street. The Squire came up beside him and said, quietly, "I'm gonna head to Gopher's for a second. You need anythin'?"

Delmar chewed on the cigar, which made his thick-rimmed glasses ride up on his cheeks; he readjusted his hat. "Bring me two Invincibles." He reached in his pocket and put two dollar bills on the counter, which the Squire put in his pocket.

"You need the Form?" the Squire asked, straight-faced.

Delmar just looked, also straight-faced, a little to the side, didn't say anything, and the Squire laughed a countrified laugh that was out of keeping with his clear, shrewd blue eyes, his dignified, thin face, and his history degree from Northwestern. He walked outside.

"What do you think C.S.A. means?" Sheila was saying. They were looking down into a case at some silver- or nickel-plated belt buckles with those letters in relief on them.

"Excuse me," Jeffrey said, looking up at Delmar.

Delmar got off the stool and walked in his side-to-side rocking limp over to the case where they were.

"We were wondering what those letters stood for."

"Those are Confederate Army belt buckles," the black

man said, sliding open the case from behind. "Confederate States of America." He set out two of them on the counter-top. The woman picked one up.

"Are they real?" she said.

"Sho' they real," Delmar said. "Look here." He took the one she had and turned it over, pointing out the maker's mark on the back, grunting a little as his mouth worked on the cigar.

Jeffrey watched Delmar's face as he showed Sheila the buckle, searching for some trace of the resentment or anger he knew must be hidden there. Sheila had stopped looking at the buckles and was surreptitiously amazed by how white Delmar's knuckles were, as if they had been cured in salt. Jeffrey was trying to figure out how old he was, but there was no telling.

Delmar put the belt buckles away. Sheila moved down the line, looking in the cases, and Jeffrey stayed there, wanting to engage the Negro in some conversation. He asked Delmar where he could hear some blues while he was in town.

Delmar, an amateur classical cellist, was more familiar with Kiri Te Kanawa than Memphis Minnie, but he knew what was expected of him in this situation. It was one of the standard roles a black had to fill where Northerners were concerned, which was to be the bearer of the Real Truth, the inside story. He said, "Go on down to Beale Street. You see all kinds of blues down there, out in Handy Park. Get you all kinds of souvenirs, anything you want."

Jeffrey, who was almost, but not quite, as square as Delmar assumed, was about to tell Delmar that he was looking

for something a little more out of the way, when he heard
Sheila say, "Oh, God," from the back of the store. A second later she said, "Oh, please," and when he looked over
he saw she was holding herself as if she were cold.

"What's the matter?" Jeffrey said. When she didn't answer, he walked around to the back where she was and
looked down into the case at a folded red flag emblazoned
with a swastika, and various inscrutable pieces of metal that
looked like armbands and medals, all with swastikas and ea-
gles on them.

"I'm sick," she said.

The bell tinkled in the front of the store and the Squire
walked back in. He laid the two cigars on the front counter
as he said to Delmar, "Winfree just popped his shoulder
out." Delmar turned toward the back of the store, and the
Squire followed his gaze back to where the two Yankees
were. He pulled out a kerchief and wiped down his face, re-
moving his half-moon glasses to wipe over the bridge of his
nose, then replacing them. The couple were coming back to
the front of the store. The young man was looking at the
ground.

"You know, that is horrible," she blurted out when she
was still ten feet away from the Squire.

"Sheila . . ." Jeffrey said.

"How can you sell those horrible things?" To the Squire
she looked as if she was about to cry; her face was all flushed
and her eyes were watery.

"Ma'am . . ." he began.

"I had relatives that were killed because of that flag. What kind of a place is this?" Her voice was loud. Delmar was looking out at the street.

"Sheila," Jeffrey said, "let's just go."

"Why are you apologizing for them?" she said to him.

"I'm not apologizing; let's just leave."

"Ma'am," the Squire said, "I'm sorry if that upset you . . ."

"*Upset* me? How can you even touch something like that? What is the matter with you?"

The Squire's face was turning bright red, but his voice was just as even as it had been. "That was a very unfortunate and misguided time, and unfortunately there have been people that felt that way about things. We sell items like that out of a historical interest. There are people who collect things like that out of a historical interest in a certain period. I'm sorry if it upset you."

She was blowing her nose into a tissue and Jeffrey put his arm around her, said, "Thank you," and guided her back out through the jingling door, into the bright afternoon.

The Squire and Delmar both watched them walk down the sidewalk, the young man talking into his wife's ear, her turning to him, stopping, obviously saying upset words to him.

"Well, goodness," the Squire said. "My goodness. They will be that way sometimes."

Delmar laughed a short, abrupt laugh, hardly more than a short, staccato hunch of his shoulders.

They were quiet for a minute or two. The Squire glanced through the paper, calming down a little. Northerners, as he had remarked countless times, saw things in black-and-white. The world was a simple place to them. Delmar was looking out the window, down the street to where the couple were still talking in agitated tones, judging by their gestures and stance. "Well, he's not gettin' any tonight," he said.

The Squire looked up from the paper. "How's that?"

"Say, he'll be coming up dry tonight," nodding down at them.

The Squire looked out at the couple, caught Delmar's meaning, and laughed. He got a big kick out of Delmar, always had. They were second cousins.

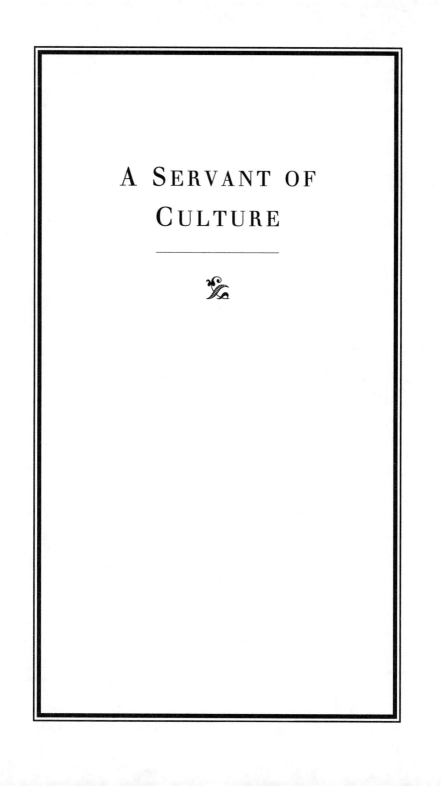

A SERVANT OF
CULTURE

Outside Arthur Golden's narrow slice of office window the snow falls past the twenty-eighth floor of the Broadcast Corporation of America building, recently purchased but not yet renamed by the Tanaka Corporation of Japan. The midtown Manhattan traffic far below on 50th Street grinds by noiselessly, drowned out by Miles Davis's "So What," playing over Golden's excellent sound system.

"Listen to Coltrane," Elliot Roth says, grinning boyishly. It is late in the afternoon, and he is paying a visit to his luckless protégé. Roth is nearing sixty-five, with wavy and pomaded gray hair, wearing a blue blazer over an avocado-colored T-shirt—a racy outfit for a man his age, but Roth, who made much money for the company when it was known as BCA Records, can do more or less what he wants. He still speaks his old-time hipster talk, blithely mixing it with a Brooks-Brothers-goes-Miami-Vice style of dress.

Over in adult pop, he is still considered a maverick. Golden sits at his desk, staring at the floor.

Elliot has found a place to rest his arm on Golden's desk, which is piled with stacks of papers, promotional photos, and cassettes in profusion, many of them demo tapes or promotional copies of things Golden is writing press releases for, or things people at other record companies send him as a courtesy. Elliot is trying to see a framed picture of saxophonist Ben Webster, leaning against the wall, on top of the junk.

Smiling, shaking his head to the music as John Coltrane finishes his solo, Elliot asks, "Where'd you get that picture of Ben? Is it one of Dave's?"

"I don't remember," Golden says. He doesn't raise his eyes.

Elliot looks at Golden. "Artie," he says, "come on, baby. It's not the end of the world. What do these *shvartzers* know about jazz, anyway?"

Golden, a heavyset man of forty, with a head of thick, gray-flecked hair, shakes his head. He sits hunched in his chair, his round shoulders humped like the trunk of a 1952 Buick. His wool tie, a concession to office protocol, is loosened around his neck; his beard conceals several patches of red, scaly eczema. His striped shirt is wrinkled at the waist, where Golden's potbelly is constantly trying to pull the tail out of his faded blue jeans. His heavy glasses are smudged. Elliot has been trying for the nine years Golden has been working at BCA to get him to dress snappier, pay more attention to his appearance, but to no avail.

"I just don't know what I'm doing here anymore," Golden says. "I'm writing press releases for a bunch of thugs and anti-Semites, and then when I try to get one project going, on someone who should be a hero to them, I get torpedoed by that snake."

"Careful, careful," Roth says, "be cool. You don't know who's listening."

"As if they don't know what I think," Golden says. "I'm a forty-year-old errand boy."

"Hey, Artie," Roth says, reaching to put his hand on his no-longer-so-young protégé's shoulder, "it's one project, man. It's one installment. You have to think more long-term."

"The long term is getting shorter every day, Elliot. I'm not twenty-five anymore."

"Hey, listen, your father's career—he should rest in peace—didn't take off until he was almost your age."

"It was a whole different world then," Artie says. "It's like comparing *Stagecoach* and *Star Wars*."

Elliot laughs and laughs at this, a big, booming laugh with vaguely hysterical overtones, for which he is famous among his colleagues, many of whom are dead from congestive heart failure. "Like comparing *Stagecoach* and *Star Wars*. That's great. I'm going to use that."

"It's yours," Golden says, fatalistically.

Five months ago, the old jazz department, run for years by a man named Ben Farber, was absorbed into the new black music department; there it now competes for attention and publicity money with funk, rap, and soul acts. Farber was eased out quickly, and Coleman Tate, an elegant, Yale-educated black in his early thirties, now directly oversees every project in the department. Two hours earlier, in a meeting with Tate, Golden's pet project idea got shot down irreversibly. It was a disillusioning blow to Golden, and an obvious harbinger of what lay in store in the future.

Arthur Golden has hoped for years to get out of publicity and into production. In particular, he has wanted to assemble a five-CD reissue set of recordings by saxophonist Lester Young, a project with extremely limited commercial appeal but unimpeachable aesthetic rationale. Ben Farber himself had promised Golden a shot as soon as the takeover question got ironed out. Of course, things didn't go as planned; Tanaka took over, the bottom line became top priority (as they liked to say), Farber was put out to pasture, and Tate came in.

It is, Golden tells himself, his own fault. He has dragged his feet for the past nine years, writing press releases, figuring he had all the time in the world to get into production. When, just after lunch, he found himself being called into Coleman Tate's office and hearing the bad news about the memo he had sent up, the realization of his situation fell on him with the weight of a heavy door being closed forever.

Tate always looks like a page out of *Gentleman's Quarterly,* in fine, wide-shouldered Italian suits, smoking cigarettes languidly and leaning back in his chair, speaking in a clipped, faintly West Indian accent. To Golden, this afternoon, he said, "Arthur, I love Lester Young. I used to play his solo from 'Taxi War Dance' on clarinet in my high school band. He was a great artist. But how can we possibly sell five CDs' worth of product on him? I have a mandate to make money here, and I would love to do it through jazz, but doing so will mean convincing our owners that there is money to be made there. If we launch a large, money-losing project, we will get off on the wrong foot."

Golden listened, growing angry. Tanaka Music, as the company was now called, had just spent close to a quarter of a million dollars promoting a single record by a rapper who sang about beating up cops and Jews. "Coleman," he said, "what was the advertising budget on Black Heat? I'm asking for less than two percent of that. I'm not saying Black Heat doesn't deserve the attention—"

Tate interrupted him, with a cryptic smile, and said, "We spend a buck to make three bucks, Artie—you should understand that." It was, Golden thought, a blatantly anti-Semitic remark, and his face had burned with frustration, although he had said nothing.

Golden wanted just to walk out, resign on the spot, but it was impossible. He and Elise had bought a house in Woodmere two years earlier, and now they had Nicole, and he wasn't about to walk out in a huff. The thing was, he didn't even hate Tate. Tate was a smart guy. At the party they'd thrown to welcome Tate to BCA, Arthur had chatted with him for a few minutes. Tate knew, it seemed, a lot about jazz; he was intimidating, too, with his expensive clothes and his working knowledge of French and German.

In principle, Golden was glad to see a black in charge of

things in a department that dealt with black music. But it rankled at the same time; his own progress had been so damnably slow. He had even noticed a strange, foreign tendency in himself at times, like an undertow; in unguarded moments, he would find himself thinking that Tate had gotten the job only because he was black, that there was a "black Mafia" at work. Then he would think to himself that that was what people used to say about Jews—probably still did—and he would feel awful. The fact that blacks and whites at the company had almost completely different cliques didn't help; groups would get quiet, guarded, when someone from the other group came around. He had been brought up to think of society's racism as "a cancer," in his father's words. Maybe, Golden thought, he should have gone over to Adult Popular with Elliot when he had had the chance.

Now Golden's office door opens and Dave Grandinetti walks in, still brushing snow off his pea coat, his camera case, and his close-cropped white hair. It is his habit to drop in unannounced, at any time. His photographs of jazz and blues players have appeared on countless album covers, although, consummate pro that he is, he is willing to photograph anything or anyone.

"They sent me over all the way to Eighth Avenue because La Hoya is supposed to be rehearsing some big thing with Prince as a guest star and the whole frigging thing is called off because of the weather," he says. "How you doing, Artie?" To Elliot, he says, "I saw Tony Bennett's man there, what's his name, Morgan. He said to call him."

"What the hell is Morgan doing over with La Hoya?"

"Do I look like Nostradamus? I don't know—getting his tool wet, probably, what do I know. Get a ginzo's tool wet and he's happy. I should know."

Golden sits, listening to Miles Davis's solo on the stereo. Even these old guys, he thinks, get out and see more than I do.

"Listen to this," Grandinetti says. "Artie, have you heard this yet? Actually, don't look at it." He pulls a CD out of his bag. "Put this on; I got it from Kathleen over at Columbia. Don't even look at it; just put it on."

Golden puts the disc into his player, presses a button, and in a moment Mahalia Jackson's voice comes out of the speakers, soaring, clear, heavy and airborne at once, singing,

"Everybody talkin' 'bout heaven ain't goin' to heaven . . ."

Golden listens in admiration; he has a weakness for black gospel music, for the absolute faith and conviction that can be found there, and which he lacks. It invariably has a purity and an assurance, a *knowing*, which places it above all the politics and bullshit of the music business, even above more secular, less disinterested forms of expression. As he listens, he actually forgets his encounter, earlier, with Tate.

Roth, across from him, grins and shakes his head. "She's so great, man. She makes me want to be a believer. The hell with *Shabbes* and bitter herbs. Right, Artie?"

"Talk about it, brother," Grandinetti says. "Hallelujah." After a moment, he adds, "I shot her at Newport in 'fifty-eight."

"Yeah?" Roth says, eyebrows arched. "Did you fuck her?"

"No," Grandinetti says. "I couldn't get past her organist."

"I'll bet she had a big organ," Roth says. They both giggle like kids.

Golden looks at them, suddenly very irritated. "Jesus," he says. "That's Mahalia Jackson. I mean . . ."

"Look at him," Grandinetti says, pointing at him. "He got religion."

"Come on," Golden says. "I mean, it's one thing to make a joke about Ella or somebody, but Mahalia Jackson is different."

Elliot is looking suspiciously at his aging protégé as if he is not sure whether to take what he is saying seriously.

Arthur looks back at him. Not in a mood to back down, he adds, "I mean, maybe she's not Barbra Streisand, but she's great"—a reference to the kinds of popular things Roth has spent his time and made his money on for years.

Roth's face gets red. "Wait a second," he begins. "Wait just a fucking second. I hope you're not saying what it sounds to me like you're saying. Who produced Joe Williams? Who took a chance on Buddy Johnson, putting him with strings? Who produced fund-raising jazz concerts for the NAACP five years in a row? Don't be so high and mighty."

Roth's eyes are wide, his face dark red, the muscles in his neck rigid, as if he is suddenly fighting for his entire life and reputation. Later this evening he will tell the others in his group therapy what happened, and how he overreacted. But now he can't stop himself. "Besides," he goes on, "how do you think they talk about us? It's 'Israelites' this, 'Jews' that . . . Did you see the *Voice* this week? The article on that son of a bitch Simmons?"

"I read it," Golden said. He is taken aback by Roth's intense reaction, but disinclined to back down. "I just—"

"And another thing, Artie—do you think anybody would be listening to Mahalia Jackson right now, or Duke Ellington, or Charlie Parker, if it wasn't for a handful of us *boychicks* running around breaking our nuts to make sure it got reissued?"

"He's right," Grandinetti says, absently paging through a trade magazine on Golden's desk.

"It's not the blacks who are out there keeping this stuff in print," Roth says.

"Well," Artie says, "they couldn't even get a job in the industry until a few years ago."

"And now that they have 'em, they're like your good friend Tate. They don't care about Bird, or Pres. They just care about exploiting their own people and making a buck, and baiting the Jews."

"All right, all right," Golden says, tired now of the grappling. "Jesus, Elliot, you get so extreme. I mean, why do you think I'm depressed? I know everything you're saying. I'm just saying to remember that Bird and Pres were black, too, right?"

Mopping his forehead with a handkerchief, Roth says, "I remember, don't worry. I've been in this business for thirty-five years. Don't worry." His hand shaking, he puts the handkerchief back in his inside blazer pocket.

"I'll tell you," Grandinetti says, trying to lighten the mood, "I've shot 'em all, and the blacks are, more often than not, the most courteous. I'd ten times over rather shoot a Dexter Gordon than a Stan Getz."

"Well, they're both dead now," Roth says. "It's the great equalizer." He stretches nervously. "What time is it, anyway?"

"Four forty-five," Grandinetti says.

"I gotta go to group." He looks over at Golden and says, "It's just one battle, Artie, not the whole war."

"I know, Elliot," Golden says. "Look, I'm sorry for yelling at you."

"I'm the one who was yelling. Don't worry about it."

"Have a good group."

After a few minutes and some desultory chatter, Grandinetti gets up and leaves, too, and Golden is alone in his office for the first time in several hours. There are two releases left to write, but he doesn't have the energy. He just sits in his desk chair, looking around his office.

It has made a decent living for him and Elise, there is no question. Somehow, though, Arthur has never been able to completely buy in and be gung ho about what he does at BCA; it embarrasses him. He didn't get involved in the music business to write press releases; he got involved because he loved jazz and blues. Jazz musicians have been his heroes since he was a kid, when his father, an entertainment lawyer, had brought him around to see all the greats. Men like Dizzy Gillespie and Count Basie had been nice to him—largely, of course, because he was David Golden's son. For a while, Arthur had even nursed hopes of becoming a jazz trumpeter.

Instead, he went to the State University of New York at Purchase, got out and was a roadie for a rock band for a while, then managed the jazz department at Sam Goody's on Sixth Avenue, finally moving to BCA, where his father's friend Ben Farber made a place for him doing jazz publicity. He went to the release parties, where now the musicians were not really as friendly—sometimes condescending, sometimes not—and Artie hung out with the others like himself—congenital outsiders, for whom jazz musicians, who could stand up onstage and spontaneously generate profound, swinging truth, represented a picture of what they themselves might have been, in an ideal world—articulate, quick-witted, admired, graceful, forceful. He collected conversations with his heroes, whom he was coming to envy as much as he loved them.

He has been telling himself for years that publicity wasn't really what he was going to do, that sooner or later he would make his move into producing, which was where the glamor was. So he didn't take his work seriously, and he was waking up now, at forty, to find out that it was, in fact, his life. The music he loved was central to him, but he was, at best, peripheral to it. Still, it was a living. And there was no denying that he liked the perks—the pictures, the books, the free CDs, the cloisonné pins, the satin windbreakers with fancy logos, the backstage passes, the invitations to parties and receptions, where he would stand around with the others, sharing scraps of information and gossip about the movers and shakers around them.

He runs his hand over his face and scratches his beard. It is time, he supposes, to go home. He puts the notes for the other releases into his backpack ("Get rid of the backpack!" Elliot had told him, two years ago), along with a few new CDs, turns off the stereo and the lights, and walks out into the hall, closing his door behind him. Jennie is still at her desk, and he says good night to her.

As he walks down the orange-carpeted, track-lit hall toward the elevators, he sees the unmistakable figure of Coleman Tate leaning against a desk, talking to one of the secretaries, elegant even in repose, in his Italian sharkskin suit. Why not, Golden thinks, use your head a little and show Coleman that there are no hard feelings.

Golden passes the elevator bay, which bisects the building, and gets a few feet farther down the hall toward Tate, then he freezes. The situation, he thinks, is awkward. He obviously is not passing just by chance; Tate knows Artie's office is on the other side of the elevators. What, he thinks, is he going to do—just walk up to them, say good night, then turn around and walk back out? He would look ridiculous.

Golden turns around and silently, quickly, pads back to the elevator bay, hoping Tate hasn't seen him skulking out. He has a plan. The floor is essentially a rectangular figure eight—two squares of hallway next to each other, sharing a side, which is where the elevators are located. He will go around the east square and approach Tate from the other side, as if he had been saying good night to someone in one of the east offices. On the way, he will think up something interesting or witty to say.

Pleased with the plan, and very nervous, he walks north through the elevator bay and makes a right. He passes one of the design departments, then rock publicity, then radio. His mind is a blank. Suddenly, passing an office where some Caribbean music is playing, he thinks of something to say. He can say, "Are you going to see Ezra Paul?" Ezra Paul is one of the new acts on Tanaka's Papaya Records subsidiary, a reggae singer, who will be appearing at the Bottom Line this evening, probably somebody Coleman likes.

Golden turns the final corner, doglegs around some boxes of product stacked up, and finds himself proceeding down the hallway toward Coleman and the secretary. As Golden approaches, Tate does not so much as look up. At the last possible moment, Golden says, "Good night, Coleman."

Tate barely raises his hand in acknowledgment. Golden walks another few steps, unsure what to do. He stops, as if he remembers something he wants to say.

"By the way," Golden begins. The "by the way" sounds stiff and artificial to him as soon as it is out of his mouth—even, perhaps, faintly imperious. Nothing to do but go on, though. "Are you going to see Ezra Paul at the Bottom Line?"

This sounds wrong, too—offhand and chatty, where Golden wants a conciliatory sound, strong but friendly. His own voice sounds unnaturally high to him, besides. He wants to convey that there are no hard feelings, not that he is cravenly hoping for some approval. . . .

Unfortunately, before Golden can figure out how to fix things, Tate says the word "Yes." He doesn't look up, and he continues talking to the secretary as if Golden isn't even there.

Golden feels as if he has just heard a pistol go off—one short, sharp, well-aimed report, then silence. He stands there stupidly for a moment, watching the secretary trying not to laugh, then, mortified, he continues down the hall to the elevators, where he turns right and punches a down button with his face flushing deep red. He feels waves of anger speeding along his nerves, like urgent messages over phone lines. He imagines that anyone could see the anger, coming off his face like heat waves off of a car hood at the beach.

The elevator door opens. Inside the car, right in front of the door, stands a black teenager supporting a handcart full of boxes. Arthur has to squeeze by him to get into the elevator; the youngster doesn't bother shifting to make room for him, and in fact ignores him completely. He should, Golden thinks, be on the freight elevator. The doors shut; the elevator drops down with a sudden free-fall, and Golden watches the back of the young man's head, where a lightning-bolt pattern has been shaved into the close-cropped hair. Everybody, he thinks, is in his own little orbit. Nobody reaches out. Breathing deeply from his stomach, Arthur says, "Long day?" trying to sound informal and comradely.

He watches the back of the black's head and, past it, the

numbers ticking off on the lighted display over the doors, showing the car's progress downward. The young man says nothing in response, and Arthur can feel his own heart swelling with rage in his chest. The elevator slows, suddenly, and alights at the eighteenth floor, where the doors open. Before the black can roll his cart out, Golden says, "Have a good night." The black still doesn't respond; he pulls back on the hand truck handle and wheels the truck out of the elevator, the doors closing just behind his heels.

The elevator drops away again, picking up speed. Golden, alone again, stares at the blinking numbers, helpless, almost choking with frustration. The absolute stony front, he thinks, the attitude. The superiority. "Nigger," he says, under his breath, as if trying it out to see what it feels like. "Nigger, nigger, nigger, nigger, nigger." After he says it, the elevator is quiet again, except for the faint whine of the cables.

Golden feels nauseous; his face feels hot. At least, he thinks, nobody heard that. The elevator slows as it approaches the ground floor, and as the doors open and the light from the brightly lit marble walls floods into the car, Golden steps forward, out into the lobby, hoping he will make it to the street without seeing anyone he knows.

MEMPHIS

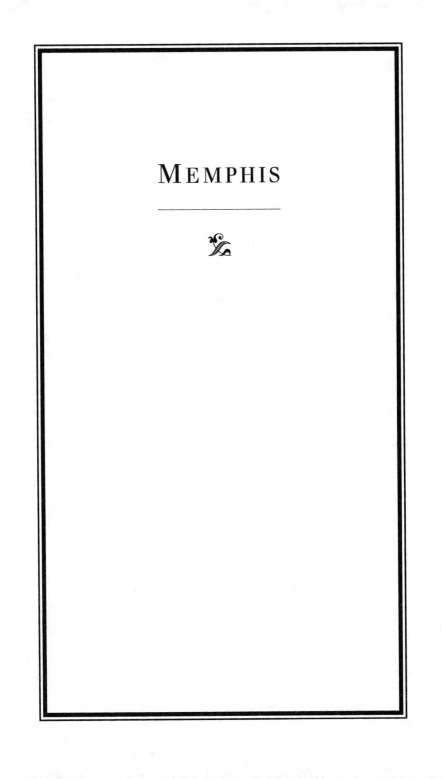

T hings went along just fine, too fine, the first couple
months I knew Suzy. Then here comes Thanksgiving. She was going home to Memphis. What's Luke
going to do. Come on to Memphis.

As soon as I said I'd come down, things changed with us.
I got a running lecture on how to dress, act, and talk down
home. Daddy was some big investment banker, and when
you head home, boy, you better have your business straight.
For two weeks before Thanksgiving, everything I did was
wrong.

Okay—this, that and the other. Don't chew gum. Don't
wear sneakers. I told her, I said, I wear about a hundred dollars' worth of clothes every day, excluding shoes, which she
knows. On the other hand, I don't stick out my little finger
when I drink a Coca-Cola, either. Oh, Luke, you're pig-
headed. Well, I'm just saying. We had about two weeks of
that.

Suzy had bright blue eyes that were always saying "Prove it." She could take care of herself. But when it came to Daddy, she got like one of these people in a religious cult. They seem as normal as potato chips until somebody mentions the guru's name and they start talking about how Swami Ding-Dong changed their life and their eyes glaze over and you can't reach them. She said he was kind of a runaround guy, lots of affairs outside the marriage. But he was supposed to be so tall and handsome that Mama put up with it. I figured maybe he fished or hunted or something. Maybe we could hop in the car and hunt up some bunnies, bring along some beers.

I'm the first one to say I don't always do too great with the parents, but I was going to make Suzy's folks like me if it was the last thing I did. I tried my best those couple of weeks before going down there. I wanted to put her mind at ease. I wore a shirt around the house, didn't eat in bed, but she was just apprehensive. I'd open a beer, and she'd be looking at me, so I'd say something like "Want to split this with me?" and she'd say something like "I hope you're not gonna get drunk on Thanksgiving." I said, "How do you figure I run a business with twelve people under me if I don't know how to handle myself?" She said, "I don't know."

I've got a good general manager, Bobby, who I can leave things with for a while at a time, so taking some extra days was no problem. The warehouse is in an area they call Death Valley. Basically it's the kind of area where you don't fall asleep with your mouth open unless you want to wake up with no teeth. But Bobby's famous for taking shit from nobody. I had some business in Cincinnati the week before Thanksgiving, and I'm from Cleveland originally, so I figured I'd drive out and spend a few days seeing everybody and then drive down to see Suzy; it's a straight shot from Cincinnati down to Memphis.

I had a great time in Cleveland. Everybody was there—Leaky Lee, Onzie, Brooks Jenkins, Meg Baker. Then I headed down to Cincinnati and the whole bunch of them came down and stayed in my hotel room, acting like a bunch of animals, as my mother used to say, and I ended up pulling into Memphis on three hours' sleep.

I got to their house sometime around three in the afternoon. They live in a brick mansion in a suburb, about an acre and a half of land around it, lots of trees. Pull it together, Luke. Suzy came outside when I drove up, and as soon as she saw me she started giving me this "How could you do this?" look. She's got blue eyes that I swear turn bottle-green when she gets mad. All she said—she didn't even kiss me—was "Mama's right inside, waitin' to meet you."

I made my way up to the front door and her mama was there, holding a drink in her left hand. She was younger than I expected, with frosted blonde hair. She said, "Hello, Mr. Jackson," with a nice smile and held open the door for me. It was a real big foyer, with a living room off to the left and a stairway with a polished wood railing curving around upstairs.

"I'm sorry Mr. Edwards isn't here right now to greet you. He had to go into town for a few hours." She had a Southern accent like a well-trimmed hedge. "Douglas is around somewhere, but you'll run into him soon enough, I'm sure." Smile. "Well, you probably want to freshen up. Suzy'll show you your room upstairs. Then come down and have a cocktail."

Suzy and I headed upstairs. All the way up, she was hissing at me, talking under her breath: "Couldn't you have gotten cleaned up at least? You smell like a *men's room.*"

"What did you want me to do? Take a shower in a water fountain someplace?" I hissed back.

"Well, why'd you have to go and get drunk for?"

"A bunch of friends came down from Cleveland. I couldn't tell them to turn around and drive back."

"I suppose they sat on your chest and poured Jack Daniels down your throat, too."

We got to the room. I set my duffel on the floor, hefted my suitcase up onto the bed, unlatched it and opened it out. "I'll be fine soon as I get a shower," I said.

She just stood there with her hands on her hips. I took off my jacket, folded it, and laid it on the bed. She just stood there.

"Hey," I said. "Come on. Aren't you even going to ask me how the trip was or anything?"

She said, "Maybe I'll think about it once you get yourself cleaned up. You better be cleaned up before Daddy gets home."

"Don't worry," I said, turning around to set my wallet and things on the bureau. I put them next to a china music box shaped like a dancing couple; they were dressed in old-fashioned pink and green costumes, like George Washington and his wife. "This is nice," I said, trying to change the subject.

"Daddy gave me that for my twelfth birthday," she said, smiling a little. Then suddenly she got a horrified look on her face.

"What's the matter?" I said.

"What did you have to bring that thing for? Jesus God Almighty." She took a step back.

I had forgotten about the gun completely. I carry it all the time when I'm on the road. It's a habit I have from the warehouse. "Forgot I even had it."

"Well, get rid of it. I thought you just kept it at the office."

"Hey—I'm carrying about ten thousand dollars' worth of materials out there in the trunk. I told you about that."

"Well, leave it outside."

"It's illegal to leave it in a car unattended."

"Not in Tennessee it ain't." I had to laugh; she was probably just faking. Had to give her credit for that. Actually, I wasn't sure myself what Tennessee law was.

"It sure as hell is," I said, bluffing. "You go check on that one more time."

"Ah'm not stayin' in this house, and my mama and daddy ain't either, till you git rid of that thang." She was regressing back to her accent, which she did when she got excited.

I just wanted a little peace. So I said, "Okay, look. Watch carefully." I pulled the gun out of the waistband of my pants, checked the chamber to make sure a round wasn't up there, then I slid the clip out.

"Okay?" I said. "You can hang on to this if you want to." I held the clip out in the palm of my hand.

"I don't even want to touch it," she said, hunching up her shoulders around her ears as if I was sticking a tarantula in her face.

"Fine," I said. "Watch." I emptied all seven rounds out of the clip and put them in my jacket pocket. Then I stuck the clip into one part of my suitcase and the body into my duffel bag. "Happy now?"

"No." She turned and walked out.

Okay. Somebody had put a stack of towels on one of the satin chairs in my room, and there was a bathroom right off the room, so I just went on ahead to get myself together. I figured once she saw me looking fresh she'd give it up. A nap was too much to ask for. If I started feeling out of it, I had some crystal meth that Onzie had given me.

I got all cleaned up and dressed, hung my jacket in the closet and headed downstairs.

Mama had a tray of hors d'oeuvres laid out on the coffee table in the living room. A thick dark green carpet covered the floor; it was like walking on a golf green. There was a fire going, crystal chandelier, all beautiful upholstered furniture. Over the fireplace they had one of those polished convex mirrors with a gold eagle on top. Mrs. Edwards greeted me with a smile. Suzy stood up, too. She had calmed down a little.

"What can I make for you, Mr. Jackson?" Mama said.

"Please call me Luke, ma'am. I'll just have whatever's handy," I said.

"Now, don't be that way," she said. "Anything you'd like, just say it."

"Well, how about a gin and tonic," I said.

"That's Mr. Edwards's drink," Mama said, smiling.

"I'll make it, Mama," Suzy said, and headed out back through a doorway.

A few paintings—portraits and hunt scenes—hung in different spots. One was a big portrait in oil of Mama.

"That was me," she said, "when I came out. I was a little debutante, only seventeen. Over there is Suzy's grandfather, Mr. Edwards's father. This small one over here is of Suzy and Rebecca. That was painted when Suzy was ten and Rebecca eight."

Suzy brought me the gin and tonic, and right then her ten-year-old brother walked into the room, wearing gray flannels, a pressed white shirt and a blue blazer, accompanied by a black nanny.

"And this is Douglas," Mrs. Edwards said.

"Hi, Douglas," I said. The nanny left the room. He was a good-looking kid. Didn't smile.

Suzy said, "Doug, this is Luke."

He walked over to me, looking me in the eye, until he was about a foot away from me. Then he socked me as hard as he could in the thigh. It hurt like hell, and I was so surprised that I yelled out "Ow!" before I checked myself.

"Douglas!" his mother said. "What kind of a way is that to behave?" Suzy had turned red as a radish. "Luke, I am sorry."

"Oh," I said, "it's no problem. Want to try that again?"

I stuck out my hand for him to shake. He took it, pumped up and down twice, like he was pumping for water, then just stood there. Not a word, through the whole thing. "All right," I said. The thigh hurt like a bastard. "You pitch for the baseball team or anything?" I asked him. "You've got a heck of a windup."

He shook his head no. Okay, I thought. That's all you get. I started to turn to Suzy and her mom, and he said, "I've got lizards."

Finally something to grab on to. "Oh yeah?" I said. "Catch 'em yourself?"

"Yeah," he said. "Wanna see 'em?"

"Don't bring out those things," Suzy said.

Mrs. Edwards added, "Maybe Luke will look at them after dinner."

I remembered what Suzy had told me, when she said she had a ten-year-old brother. "He's crazy."

"All ten-year-olds are crazy," I had said.

"Maybe he's just kind of wild, then. I don't think Daddy and Mama expected him. There's seventeen years between him and Becky. Daddy hasn't got the heart to crack the whip on him like he should."

Just then Mr. Edwards swept into the room from the kitchen, wearing a gray topcoat. He was skinny and tall, clean shaven, with gray hair waved and pomaded. Mama and Suzy looked like the President of the United States had just walked in.

"Frances," Mrs. Edwards said.

"Hello, darling," he said. He leaned down and kissed her

on the mouth and held it for a couple of seconds. Suzy was looking at me expectantly, and I gave her a wink.

When he was finished with Mama, he turned to Suzy and said, "Hello, sweet." She turned her cheek to him and he kissed it.

"Daddy, this is Luke."

"Yes. Welcome, sir. It's a pleasure to meet you. Have these girls been taking good care of you?"

"Just fine, sir," I said, shaking his hand. "Thank you." His face was thin, with high cheekbones, and his hands were manicured. He had Suzy's flashing blue eyes, and skin you could almost see through. He was no outdoorsman. Definitely a dinner-party playboy.

"Well," he said, taking off his topcoat, which Suzy took from him and went to hang up, "do you need a refresher?" I had gone through my whole drink.

"Yes, thanks," I said.

"Gin and tonic?"

I nodded, and he said, "Splendid. That's my drink, too." We walked together toward the bar, behind the couch and under the portrait of Suzy and her sister.

He handed me a fresh drink. It was almost straight gin. He took a long pull on his, with his eyes closed. "Have you ever had this?" He pulled up a bottle of gin of a brand I'd never heard of, from India.

We sat down on the couch, which I sank into like it was a marshmallow. I told him a little about the trucking business, which he seemed to be interested in hearing about. He had a funny way of listening; it was like he was reading my lips. Doug had disappeared; so had Suzy and Mrs. Edwards. I figured they were in the kitchen.

"You know, I've always loved to travel," he said. "I feel at times as if I've had quite a sedentary life, although goodness knows we've gotten around. We visited Burma last year. Strictly vacation. I was there for a week before Anna joined me. Quite good sport," he said, flashing his blue eyes at me.

"Were you hunting or fishing at all?"

"My Lord, no. I did some fishing as a boy, but I don't think I'd know one end of the rod from the other today. The fishing rod, that is. As far as hunting, I never have tried it. I have been reading the biography of Hemingway by this man Berger. Have you read it?"

"No, sir," I said.

"Call me Cap, please. No, I am quite fascinated by that kind of a life—shooting and drinking and going to Africa and all that. I'm more of a tennis player, I suppose you'd say. Do you play tennis?"

"I've done it a few times," I said. "I'm not too great at it."

"How long will you be staying with us? Perhaps we'll play some tomorrow."

"I guess through the weekend, if that's okay."

"Stay the month, son. Anna," he called out. "Anna."

Mrs. Edwards came in from the kitchen. "Yes, darling."

"Do we have that time booked at the Reserve tomorrow? Mr. Jackson and I are going to play some tennis."

"I think we have the three o'clock time, as usual. What a nice idea. Are you a tennis player, Luke?"

"As I just told Mr. Edwards, I haven't really played much. I know how, though."

"Well, I'm sure you'll have a good time. I think that's lovely. I'll call the Reserve and double-check the time, Frances. Dinner will be served in about two minutes; Mayanne is just putting the finishing touches on the salad."

"Wonderful," Dad said as she left the room. "I'm a very lucky man," he said with a satisfied smile. He stood up. "Have a refresher?"

"No, thanks, sir; I'm doing fine," I said. I was pretty much whacked.

"And please call me Cap," he said, pouring himself another stiff one. "You make me feel antediluvian."

Before we went in to dinner I figured I'd go upstairs and throw some water on my face again, and I excused myself. So far, so good, I thought. Daddy seemed to like me. That was what was important. Suzy had gotten real daughterly, polite, didn't say hardly anything. I kept looking at her like, "How am I doing?" but it was Daddy's show all the way. That was fine, though. The alcohol factor was a little hard to believe.

When I got to my room, Douglas was standing outside the door, staring up at me.

"Hey, Douglas," I said. "How ya doin'?"

"I'm not Douglas," he said. This kid, I thought, is full of surprises.

"Sorry about that. Who are you?"

"I'm Dick Tracy."

75

"Okay, Dick," I said. "I'm going to wash my hands before dinner. How about you?"

"No," he said, taking a step backward.

"Okay," I said. I walked into my room and left the door open and he followed me in and sat on the bed. I looked at him in the mirror as I was washing my hands; he was just sitting there watching me like I was the first halfway exciting thing that had happened in months. "I bet it gets pretty lonely around here sometimes, huh?" I said. Then I added, "Dick?"

He nodded his head up and down exaggeratedly. "Can we go on an adventure?" he said.

Adventure, I thought. "Sure," I said. "What kind of adventure?"

"Let's go in my parents' room and search for evidence."

"Hmmmm," I said. I dried my hands and walked back into the room. He was looking around at my stuff. I felt sorry for him. He was stuck here with his mom, his nanny, and his father, who was definitely a mixed message as a role model. They probably never paid any attention to him. He needed somebody to take him around and show him how to do guy stuff.

"I tell you what," I said, "why don't we go eat, and maybe later on we can go outside and I'll show you some wrestling moves." We could do them on the lawn. If Suzy didn't like it, tough.

"No," he said, with a whine in his voice. "I want to have an adventure."

"Okay," I said. He looked like he was getting cranked up

to throw a shit fit. "We've got to go eat first, though. After dinner we'll go off someplace and have an adventure. Okay?" He nodded kind of absently. "Come on, Dick," I said. "Go on get ready for dinner."

We walked out of the room and I closed the door. He ran down the hall and I walked downstairs. Dougy was a tough case, no question about that. Daddy and Suzy were still talking in the living room. As soon as I got there, Mrs. Edwards came out and called us to the table. We walked through the foyer, into the big dining room, where a table had been set under a chandelier. The silverware was sparkling. Daddy was going to sit at the head of the table nearest the kitchen, Suzy on the left nearest the foyer, and Mrs. Edwards on the right. I was seated at the opposite end, with my back to a large bay window. It was dark out. There was one place open, on Suzy's side, next to Daddy.

"Olive," Mrs. Edwards said. In a moment the nanny appeared. "Can you tell Douglas to come to the table, please."

With that, Douglas ran around the corner and into the room.

"Douglas, don't run in the house," Mrs. Edwards said.

"Where'd you get off to?" Olive said.

"Look what I found," Douglas said. His hair had gotten messed up and he was minus the blazer. He opened both hands and revealed, with everybody craning to look, two hands full of bullets. Everything stopped.

After a second or two, Mrs. Edwards said, "Where in God's name did you get those things?" She looked at Olive and said, "Has Wendell been by here again?"

"No, ma'am," Olive said. "I haven't even talked wit' him." Then, to Douglas, she said, "Where'd you get those at?" Mr. Edwards was frowning slightly, staring at the bullets.

"I found them in a coat hangin' in one of the closets," he said.

"What coat?" Mrs. Edwards said. "No one in this house owns a gun. I want to know where you got those."

This wasn't a good situation. I had to say something. Make it good, Luke. "I better explain," I said.

I told them about how I have to carry the gun for work, and about Death Valley. Just so they didn't think I was blowing things out of proportion, I told them about the time three guys broke in the back windows and Bobby got one of them spread-eagled facedown on the ground, with his magnum pointed at the back of his head, and made the guy's friends stack up a whole afternoon's worth of boxes. I almost told them the pit bull story, but I figured they might not be ready for that one. Then I said I had taken the gun apart upstairs and put the bullets in the jacket pocket. I said the bullets had probably just fallen out and Dougy must have just found them on the floor.

"I found 'em right in your pocket," Dougy said, suspiciously, as if I was trying to get away with something. "They didn't fall out."

They sat there staring at me for a minute or two, except for Suzy, who wouldn't look at me. I figured maybe they might be a little embarrassed that their son had gone through my stuff, but that didn't seem to occur to them.

———

"Mr. Jackson, I have a request to make," Mr. Edwards said. "I'd very much appreciate it if you would keep the weapon outside in the trunk of your car. I'll take full responsibility on the unlikely event that something happens and the gun is discovered there while you are here."

"I'd be glad to do that. I brought it in without really thinking." I started to get up.

"No, no . . . please wait until after dinner. Yes, sit down. Thank you."

We just sat there and ate. I tried to catch Dougy's eye, but he had gotten quiet and stayed busy eating. Nobody talked. Every once in a while, Daddy's eyes would flick up from the tablecloth to my face and focus. But most of the time he just sat there with his finger across his lip. Suzy was treating me like I was a complete stranger.

I tried to think if there was any way to make things better. After a while I gave up on that and thought about mixed nuts for some reason. I started thinking about what the best nuts were, in order. You have cashews, peanuts, almonds, pecans, Brazil nuts, and the little round ones. Filberts. Then I had this thought that they were like the properties in Monopoly. Like peanuts were the slums, almonds were the light blue ones, filberts were the railroads, then cashews were the red ones, pecans were Marvin Gardens, and Brazil nuts were Boardwalk and Park Place. After that, I tried to remember the names of everybody in the Addams Family.

After dinner we went into the living room for coffee. Everyone was still acting uncomfortable. Suzy was avoiding looking at me, like I had herpes of the eyeballs. Finally

I figured things weren't going to get any better the way they were headed, so I said, "Look, I'll be glad to do whatever I can to get things back on track so we don't have to sit here staring at the rug all night. Like I said, I carry it in my job. I wish I didn't have to, but that's where I am."

Everybody just looked at me kind of surprised for a minute. Suzy licked her lips and looked through me. Mrs. Edwards smoothed her dress and looked at Daddy-o and said, "I think we're not too used to this sort of thing. Nobody's blaming anything on you Luke; I think we were just a bit taken aback."

"Maybe we ought to play a game or something. We could loosen up," I said. After a second or two, Mrs. Edwards said, "Well . . . that might be a good idea. Suzy, do you still have your Parcheesi board upstairs that you and Rebecca used to play on all the time with Papa?"

"Whatever happened to conversation, I'd like to know," Daddy said. Everybody looked at him now. He had really been putting away the wine at dinner, and now I realized he was looped. "We're not really game players, I suppose, Mr. Jackson."

"Does that mean we're not playing tennis tomorrow?" I said.

"Tennis is a sport, not a game."

"Hey, I tell you what," I said, "I hear you're kind of a sport yourself."

Nobody said anything. Daddy's face turned the color of boiled shrimp. Come on, I thought, say something smartass. This was more fun than staring at the rug. Old Olive was standing by the door of the living room, and I lifted my cup to her. She didn't move a muscle in her face, just turned and walked away.

Right about then I began to think about where I would spend the night. There had to be millions of small hotels in Memphis, and I figured I'd just take off, probably. This whole thing had started on the wrong foot, and it was going to stay there. It was just bad luck, and probably wasn't supposed to work out. I said, "Excuse me for a minute," and got up like I was going to the john.

Upstairs I got my stuff out of the bathroom and threw it in the duffel. It had started raining outside; I wouldn't have to drive too far, at least. I put a few other things back in the suitcase, including a sweater she had given me for my birthday. I checked the dresser drawers, then I pulled my jacket out of the closet and looked around some more to make sure I wasn't leaving anything. I checked the nightstand one last time. Then I just stood there for a minute or two. I felt like I could take off my tie for the first time since the whole Thanksgiving business came up. I had crossed the line and there was nothing left to worry about. I wasn't particularly happy about it. I wondered how anybody ever worked anything out. Learning how to be with someone was like leaving a trail of crumbs leading into the woods; the storm comes and blows the trail away, and next time you have to make the same exact mistakes. I saw myself in a small, chilly hotel room off a fluorescent-lit corridor, trying to sleep and listening to the retching of the ice machine down the hall.

Right then Suzy walked into the room, without knocking,

which is standard. I started zipping up the zippers on my bags.

"I'm packing as fast as I can," I said.

She stood there watching me; I could feel her eyes on the side of my head. The room had gotten hotter.

"You," she said, in a hoarse voice, more like a croak, "aren't going anywhere."

I looked up at her; her eyes were puffy, like she'd been crying. "What are you talking about?" I said. "Your mama and daddy think I'm some kind of serial killer."

Her lips were pressed tight together, and she didn't look at me. Instead she reached over to the bureau, picked up the china music box I had noticed earlier and, grimacing, threw it; it grazed the nightstand, then it hit the floor, breaking, behind the bed. "They'll get over it," she said, in a raw voice, looking at me now as if she thought I was playing dumb and forcing her to tell me something I already knew. "It ain't the end of the world."

RESPONSIBILITY

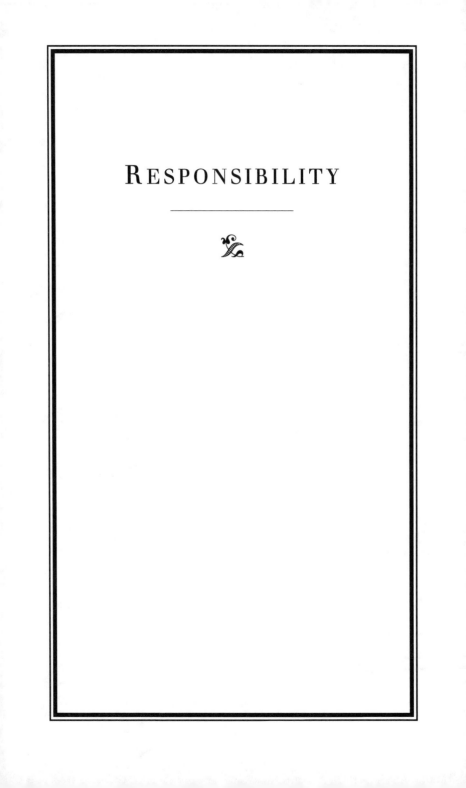

P eter Schneider unwrapped a turkey club sandwich in the passenger seat of the truck's cab, kicking an empty soda can out of the way as he settled himself. Next to him, behind the wheel, Peter Kiezlow carefully opened a thin plastic tray containing a chef's salad. They had parked on lower Broadway near New York University, two blocks from Washington Square. It was early October, still warm despite the Halloween decorations in shop windows, and the sight, from the high perch of the truck, of book-laden students hurrying by put Schneider in a reflective mood. He and Kiezlow had themselves graduated from college two years before, and Schneider had lately been allowing himself to feel old.

"That guy earlier reminded me of Ethan Schlinger," Schneider said.

"What guy?" Kiezlow said. He was studying the contents of his tray with a placid frown.

" 'It's rocking,' " Schneider said. They sometimes referred back to customers by some characteristic phrase the customer had uttered. An older Chinese man to whom they had delivered a sofa that morning, for example, was "Want lemonade?" "It's rocking" was a young man who lived in a bare apartment in one of the new high rises nearby; they had delivered an armchair and a couch to him the day before, and he had called the office complaining that the armchair rocked on his floor. When they stopped back that morning, before lunch, Kiezlow slid the armchair two inches to the side on the polished parquet, and it was solid. "It's your floor," Kiezlow said as they went for the door. The young man stood there sheepishly as they left; he hadn't tipped them on either occasion.

"Who is Ethan Schlinger?" Kiezlow said.

"The pre-med you hit with the water balloon when we were juniors. The one who kept asking Sue Harris out? You got his books wet and he said, 'You'll pay for these. . . .' " Schneider warmed to the memory; chiding, he said, "What are you, senile?"

He regretted this as soon as he said it, although Kiezlow's face registered nothing negative. After a moment, Kiezlow laughed appreciatively, and Schneider felt relieved. He filled the moment by biting into his sandwich. Since his friend's breakdown nine months before, Schneider had felt uncomfortable with him; Kiezlow had improved enough so that it was easy to forget what he had been through. His mind was still a little dim, like headlights in a car with a weak battery, but recognizable in flashes.

Responsibility

An odd and consuming caution seemed to have taken him over. The manifestations of it irritated Schneider in a way he was not proud of but couldn't seem to help. Small things, like Kiezlow's intense preoccupation, earlier, with finding a legal parking spot for the truck during lunch. "Double-park it," Schneider had said. "What are they going to do? Tow the truck?" Kiezlow ignored him; his care with such details seemed to Schneider to be the mirror image of the side of him that had once issued in audacious and extremely detailed pranks and jokes.

They were both outsiders at the small New England college they had attended—Schneider a New York Jew and Kiezlow a Jesuit-educated Pole from the Bronx, whose family had escaped from the Nazis by way of England after selling everything they owned. Kiezlow had always had a self-assurance that allowed him to perform the most outrageous acts with a bravura that charmed almost everyone, and which Schneider envied and loved. He could get people to do things. Once, at college, he had organized twenty people, all holding pies, to hide in doorways and behind trees around the green next to the freshman dining hall. It was their classmate Dick Chandler's birthday, and Kiezlow had conscripted another friend to meet Chandler for lunch, walk him halfway across the green, and then run away. Kiezlow, dressed in a Union Civil War tunic rented for the occasion, read "The Charge of the Light Brigade" over a walkie-talkie to the three other group leaders while they all waited. The friend did her job perfectly, and at the moment she ran away, Kiezlow's troops descended on Chandler from all cor-

ners of the green, hollering and holding pies aloft. Outma-
neuvered on every side, Chandler dove onto the lawn, where
he was covered with pies. A few moments later, President
Weeks appeared unexpectedly, walking along the path with
one of the college's trustees. Kiezlow, wearing his Civil War
uniform, strode up and greeted him, and they chatted for
several moments. The president even congratulated him on
a successful campaign.

Kiezlow was regarded as the most promising poet at the
college. He was tall and strongly built, with sandy hair and
a sculpted face with blue eyes that were always alert, or had
been. Schneider was half a head shorter, with tightly wound
black curly hair and a round, prominent nose that formed
the centerpiece of a boyish, credulous expression. He, too,
was trying to write poetry, but he lacked Kiezlow's outgo-
ing nature, and he became a happy acolyte. They could
often be seen in a corner at parties, Kiezlow talking to
Schneider with broad gestures about the theory of history
in Ezra Pound's Cantos, or about the relation between Pico
della Mirandola and Dante, while Schneider listened in-
tensely, nodding and frowning. They went on road trips,
gave readings, drove all night to Florida during spring break.
Kiezlow always had a plan, of some sort, and Schneider was
always ready to follow.

After graduation, Kiezlow supported himself working in
the box office of a small West Side theater. He would call
Schneider in the evenings, and they would go out to Greenwich Village bars, where Kiezlow would hold forth on literature, describing plans for projects—a biography of Ezra

Pound, a science-fiction trilogy—in stunning detail, and Schneider would listen, wishing he commanded such eloquence.

But as the year went on, Schneider began to have the uneasy feeling that Kiezlow was losing control. Kiezlow never showed Schneider anything he was working on, and he reacted badly when pressed to do so. He was also smoking a lot of marijuana. At a New Year's party, less than a week before Kiezlow broke down, they shared a joint and Kiezlow claimed that he was James Joyce reincarnated, and that he had plans to translate *Ulysses* into Polish. "I thought you were writing a science-fiction trilogy," Schneider said, before he thought. Kiezlow stopped talking, looked at him with an amazed expression, as if he had just uncovered a network of treachery, said, "Fine," and walked away. Neither ever mentioned the incident again.

Kiezlow looked different now, thinner, almost translucent. He had lost weight in the hospital, and his face had become even more sculpted. Schneider had gone to visit him only once while he was there, with a few of their classmates. They spent an uneasy half hour in Kiezlow's cell-like room, overlooking a gloomy courtyard from a high, barred window on Manhattan's Upper East Side. Kiezlow sat quietly on his single bed the entire time, occasionally laughing at something someone would say. At one point, a strange woman entered the room uninvited, wearing an orange T-shirt down the front of which streams of spilled food had left their stains. Walking slowly, as if through waist-deep water, she approached Kiezlow, pushed him back on the bed, and started kissing him. Kiezlow offered no resistance, and nobody knew what to do. An orderly eventually came in and led her out. Kiezlow lay there afterward, staring at the ceiling; Schneider and the others sat wordlessly, afraid even to look at one another.

Kiezlow got out of the hospital after a couple of weeks, but Schneider began avoiding his friend. They would run into each other occasionally at parties, where Kiezlow seemed like a ghost of himself. The hospital visit had been profoundly disturbing to Schneider. He had, in various ways, relied on Kiezlow to provide an image of something like grandeur, to which he could aspire. The notion that one's role could be altered that precipitously frightened him, as if such instability might, in some way, rub off.

Still, Kiezlow's absence hung over Schneider like a bird of ill omen. His own life wasn't going so well; he held down a succession of odd jobs while trying to write his poetry, borrowed money from his parents—floundered, in short. The amniotic fluid of invulnerability that had seemed to surround him had evaporated. He found himself worrying about things in ways he never had. For a couple of months that summer, Schneider lived off the money he'd made from a phone sales job that spring. He spent his days walking around Greenwich Village, writing in cafés, imagining the scenes of his days as photographs in some future biography of himself, but at the end all he had to show was a crumpled pocket notebook, with some fragmentary lines and copious journal entries. By September he needed a job again. He had heard, through friends, about Kiezlow delivering furniture, and when things got down to the wire, he decided to call him.

The month on the truck was the first real time they had spent together since Kiezlow's breakdown. Kiezlow didn't seem as drugged and absent as he had a few months earlier, but neither was he the same as he had been before the breakdown. Schneider occasionally tried to re-create the kinds of conversations they had once had, but Kiezlow didn't have much to say. Schneider quickly became restless with the work itself. To him it was a necessary evil, a way to make some money, but Kiezlow seemed to take it seriously, and this disturbed Schneider. As the month went by and Schneider rode above the heads of pedestrians and the roofs of taxi cabs, he began to feel separated from the world, an onlooker, sidelined from the main game. He longed for an old intensity that he feared might elude him forever.

"Do you want these egg slices?" Kiezlow asked him now.

"No," Schneider said, balling his sandwich wrapping paper up. They were finished.

"Time to head north with the big rigs," Kiezlow said.

"Where's the next one?"

"Nyack," Kiezlow said, closing his plastic tray.

Schneider took their bags and papers and descended onto the sidewalk to find a trash can as Kiezlow started the truck. Standing on the sidewalk, surrounded by the sunlight and the people going places, Schneider felt an urge to bolt, to stay on the ground and walk away toward Bleecker Street. He wanted to go to a café where the NYU undergraduates would be drinking espresso, and kill the afternoon walking around Washington Square Park. After a moment he climbed back up into the truck.

"I wish we had a joint to smoke," he said, more out of perversity than anything. He knew very well that marijuana had been a destabilizing element for Kiezlow.

"That could be arranged," Kiezlow said.

Schneider looked at his friend. "Are you serious?"

"I'm not serious," Kiezlow said, "but I have marijuana."

"Since when have you been smoking again?"

"Just once in a while," Kiezlow said.

Schneider felt faint hoofbeats of anxiety in his stomach. "Did you want to smoke it here?" he asked.

"I would prefer not to," Kiezlow said. "Let's head out for the Nyack run and do it on the way." Kiezlow looked out the driver's window back at the oncoming traffic, then eased the truck out again down Broadway.

They lit the joint on the Henry Hudson Parkway, once they were safely away from Manhattan and its police and possible mishaps. Schneider had rolled it, and Kiezlow had been highly cautionary about spillage, any evidence left in the cab. It was a miserable, wilted joint, but it was good, fresh leaf, and they were high by the time they were ten minutes out of the city. The parkway's bellows were in full autumn blow, luminous red and orange and yellow leaves, backlit and filled by the sun. When they emerged from the leafy precincts of the parkway to cross the Tappan Zee Bridge, the bright October sky was ridged with translucent, banded white clouds. The water spangled on the Hudson River, and the traffic across the Tappan Zee seemed to

Schneider like the moving pulse of life itself.

"Heading north with the big rigs," Kiezlow said.

"Move 'em out," Schneider said. For the first time in a long while he felt the sense of lift that had always characterized their time together. Instead of a jail cell, the truck's cab felt like a tree house from which they could look out at the world in perfect control. Schneider felt an overwhelming tenderness toward everything, as well as a sense of limitless entitlement. Memories of old road trips, with Kiezlow piloting him through the unexpected, warmed him again, the feeling of the world favoring him. He wanted the ride to go on forever.

"Let's drive to Canada," he said.

Kiezlow, squinting out the windshield, said, "We can't: We have the Riverdale delivery after this."

Schneider frowned; he wondered if Kiezlow had heard him correctly. Kiezlow drove with a flat expression on his face. The serious response puzzled Schneider; it was a false note. "Come on," Schneider said. "Let's just dump the stuff and live in the truck."

"I'm responsible for the truck."

Schneider looked across the seat at his friend. Kiezlow's hair, light brown and fine as a baby's, was blowing around in the breeze from the open window. His refusal to participate in the fantasy annoyed Schneider. In a teasing way that went back to their college days, Schneider said, "You're getting old."

Kiezlow kept looking out the windshield. After a moment he turned to Schneider and said, "I do what I have to

do. Don't rely on me to supply adventure in your life."
Then he turned his head and looked back out the window.

Schneider felt as if he had been struck in the face. He
couldn't locate an appropriate response. The implication
that he was being fatuous left him completely defenseless.
As suddenly as his good mood had come on, it had dissipated. His face felt hot, and he looked out at the parkway
now, hardly seeing anything.

It took twenty minutes after the Tappan Zee to find the place
of the delivery, a boarding school just outside of Nyack.
Kiezlow said nothing the whole way, and Schneider felt
completely adrift. The town itself, which they passed
through, was pretty and contained, and it reminded Schneider, pleasantly, of college. He admired the little shops and
luncheonettes and cafés, as the truck shouldered its way
through the narrow, dappled streets. They passed a sta-
tionery store, called Bogart's, with a long window full of
black cat and witch cutouts. He wanted things to be okay
again.

"Everything is Halloween up here," he said, hoping to
break the ice.

"What's the name on the order form, at the school?"
Kiezlow replied, pointing to an envelope on the dashboard.

Schneider looked at it and said, "Mrs. Ziebarth." Kiezlow
was not going to let go, Schneider thought. He wished he
could erase it and just enjoy being out of the city. But if
Kiezlow was going to be that way, he thought, there was

nothing he could do. He felt himself sliding deeper into gloom.

They found the school, a small compound five minutes outside of town. Kiezlow pulled the truck over, swung himself down from the cab, slammed the door and started for the main building almost in one motion, holding the order papers in his hand. Schneider, slower getting out, followed. The grounds were very quiet.

The school's main building was two stories high and looked to Schneider to have been built in the 1950s. They entered through the industrial blue doors at the end of one of the building's three wings, which formed a giant T on the grounds. The hallway they entered was darkened; its glazed cinderblock walls reflected pale light from the open doors of empty classrooms. Kiezlow strode purposefully down the hall, and Schneider hurried to catch up, saying, "Where are we going?"

"We're going to find the office."

"Maybe we should ask somebody."

"Do you see anyone to ask?"

The hallway ended in a T, and Kiezlow turned right, leading the way. This hall opened out shortly into a wide lobby with polished terrazzo floors, well lit by the sunlight from outside. They found the office, opposite broad doors that opened into an auditorium, walked in, and stood at a waist-high reception desk.

"Where is everybody?" Schneider asked.

A short woman with gray hair stepped tentatively out from a door that led to another room; her expression was perplexed, quizzical. "May I help you?" she said in a small, reedy voice.

"Are you Mrs. Ziebarth?" Kiezlow said.

"No, sir," the woman said. "I'm Mrs. Holley. Mrs. Ziebarth is on vacation. Is there anything I can do for you?" She looked from one of their faces to the other; her head shook just a little. Her gray hair was carefully permed, and thinning, and she wore a nubby red blazer with a marcasite cat pinned to the lapel.

"We're delivering six beds from Handle With Care furniture."

The woman frowned, raised her eyebrows, looked down at the desk for a moment as if she had just misplaced something, then back up at them. "Oh?" she said. "I haven't heard anything about that. Beds?" She looked back and forth at them, apprehensively.

Schneider began to feel as if he was going to have to laugh. Kiezlow looked serious. "Mrs. Ziebarth put in an order for six beds. Here," he said, handing her the paper, "is the order form."

She read the form as if she were reading a telegram containing urgent but confusing instructions, her mouth shaping indistinct words as she read. She pressed her lips together, then said, "I'm not authorized to accept this. I don't even know which dormitory the beds are for." She looked up at them with an amazed expression.

Kiezlow looked at her evenly and impassively. "Is there anyone else here who might know?"

"Oh, no," she said, arching her eyebrows again. "They

all went down to the Bronx Zoo. We're a small school, only fifty boys. They all went down to the Bronx Zoo. Mr. Tuttle went with them. I'm sorry."

Kiezlow looked at her evenly and impassively. After a moment, he said, "May I use a telephone?"

"Certainly," she said, her head shaking a little more. "I realize this must be an inconvenience. . . . Come around; you can use either of those. . . ."

Kiezlow went around the desk to one of the smaller desks and picked up one of the phones, leaving Schneider at the desk with Mrs. Holley. Schneider was relieved that it seemed they wouldn't have to make the actual delivery. Beds were the hardest thing they had to deliver; the frames all had to be assembled with bolts, and it took a long time. He was glad the school couldn't take them.

"It's terrible when things like this happen," Mrs. Holley said to him.

"Oh, it's okay," he said. "It means less work." He smiled an ingratiating smile at her, and her head went back slightly and tilted to one side, as if she were considering a dubious proposition.

"Man makes his living by toil," she said.

"Well, yeah," he said, hoping he hadn't offended her.

"I'm seventy-nine years old," she said. "I just volunteer here, since Mr. Holley died three years ago."

"What kind of school is this?" he asked her. Kiezlow was finishing on the phone; Schneider thought he looked unhappy.

"It's a school for boys," she said, her eyebrows arching

97

again, and her head nodding. "They're taught the importance of work and nature, and given a full course of study."

Kiezlow came back around the desk. "When will Mrs. Ziebarth be back from her vacation?" he said.

"Not until next week," the lady said, nodding, adjusting her high-necked blouse. "I'm very sorry I can't help you."

"Do you have any idea which dormitory the beds were intended for?" he asked her. Schneider looked at his face for a moment, thinking, This woman doesn't know anything; let's get out of here.

She frowned a private frown and said, "No, sir, as I said; I'm very sorry."

"Is there any guarantee that if we attempt the delivery again next week that the same thing won't happen?"

"A guarantee?" she said, looking faintly alarmed. "I can ask Mr. Tuttle when he gets back. . . ."

"Let's go," Schneider said.

Kiezlow turned to look at him, his eyes wide and questioning. "Those who evade responsibility must abide by the decisions of those who assume it," he said.

"But she doesn't know anything," Schneider said. "She's just minding the store."

Turning back to the woman, Kiezlow said, "Would you agree with this assessment?"

"I'm just volunteering," she said. "I told this gentleman before."

"Just volunteering?" Kiezlow said. "Is that an excuse to waste people's time?"

Schneider was getting a bad feeling. The woman's cheeks

were a pale pink now, and her head tremor was more pro-
nounced. "Come on, Peter," Schneider said, gently taking
Kiezlow's arm. Kiezlow threw off Schneider's hand, spun
around and walked out of the office.

Schneider said, "I'm sorry for this."

"He seems quite upset," the woman said.

"Don't worry about it," Schneider said. Then he left the
office, too.

Kiezlow pulled the truck over in front of Bogart's, in Nyack.
They hadn't spoken as they drove back into the town, but
now Schneider said, "What are you doing?"

"I'll be back in a minute," Kiezlow said, turning off the
ignition and exiting the cab. Schneider watched him walk
around the front of the truck and into Bogart's. His friend's
behavior made him nervous, and he wished there were another way to get back into the city easily. For a moment he
thought of commandeering the truck himself. But even had
it been a practical idea to begin with, Schneider couldn't
drive a standard shift, much less maneuver a truck of that
size. He contented himself with looking out the windshield
at the golden light in the trees on the shaded street.

Kiezlow came out of Bogart's carrying a brown paper
bag. He opened the driver's door and climbed into the cab.
"Fear and loathing in Nyack," he said.

"What did you get?" Schneider asked.

From out of the bag, Kiezlow carefully drew two cheap
Halloween face masks, one of some kind of fairy princess,

with a tiara and yellow hair, and one of Ronald Reagan. "Last year's model," Kiezlow said.

"That's nice, Peter," Schneider said. "What are those for?"

Kiezlow slipped the Reagan mask on. "For Halloween."

Schneider looked at the other mask, which Kiezlow was holding out for him. "Thanks a lot," he said. "I get to be the fairy princess?"

Kiezlow looked at him through the slit eyes of the Reagan mask.

"What am I supposed to do with this?" Schneider said.

"Put it on."

For a moment, Schneider had the sense that time itself was accelerating; it was an odd, vertiginous feeling that he recognized as the adrenaline rush belonging to the moments when he could get swept up in a plan, and Kiezlow suddenly had a plan. Schneider imagined the expressions on people's faces seeing the truck moving through the streets, piloted by Ronald Reagan and a fairy princess. Kiezlow seemed to have forgotten their unpleasant exchange. Maybe, Schneider thought, they could get past it after all and have some fun. He put the mask to his face and pulled the rubber band back over his head, adjusting it for comfort in his curly hair. The smooth, brittle surface of the mask pressed up against his nose and cheeks and the rims of his eyes.

"It's too tight," he said, rolling down the passenger window to get a look at himself in the side-view mirror. The effect was undeniably humorous. He looked back across the seat at Kiezlow. The Reagan mask was crude but accurate;

the brush of brown plastic hair at the top of the mask was shiny and striated.

Kiezlow turned his face forward and started the truck, and they pulled out down the main street. Schneider noticed a woman pushing a baby stroller, smiling uncertainly and pointing at them. They turned right at the next corner, then again at the next, and the next; one or two more people noticed them and pointed. When they approached the main street again, Kiezlow made a left and headed back in the direction of the school.

"Where are we going?" Schneider asked.

Kiezlow stared straight ahead, shifting gears expertly. " 'Whatever is profound loves masks,' " he said. "We abide by the local traditions."

Sitting in the passenger seat, wearing the mask, Schneider wished he knew what they were doing, but they were on a mission of some sort, and he decided that was enough for him, especially if it meant delaying work.

Kiezlow wheeled the truck through the gates of the school grounds, pulled into a small parking area and cut the engine.

"What are we doing?" Schneider asked.

"We're going to pay Mrs. 'I Can't Help You' a visit," Kiezlow said, picking up the bag that had contained the masks. He opened his door and stepped down onto the ground. Schneider got out, too, and met Kiezlow around the front of the truck.

"What are you talking about?" Schneider said. "What about the other delivery?"

"We have time," Kiezlow said. "We'd still be assembling

beds." From out of the bag he pulled two small black plastic toy handguns. He held one out to Schneider, butt first, and Schneider felt a swell of fear in his stomach. It was impossible to read Kiezlow's expression through the eye slits.

"What are you going to do? Hold her up?" Schneider's face was sweating under his mask. He looked at the mask of Ronald Reagan with Kiezlow's eyes looking out at him, and he had the eerie sense that his friend had gone crazy.

"Listen, Peter," Schneider said, taking off the mask, "this isn't a good idea. We can't do this. All right? Let's just get back in and do the last delivery and go home, man. Come on."

Kiezlow watched him silently, and Schneider began to feel very spooked. Around them the afternoon sky had grown overcast, and occasional leaves tumbled past in the breeze.

"Peter," Schneider said. "Say something."

After a moment, Kiezlow took off the Reagan mask. He stood there with it in his hand and regarded Schneider with an appraising look.

"What?" Schneider said.

"You're making a decision?" Kiezlow said. "Or are you asking me to make a decision?"

Schneider didn't know what to say, because he didn't know the answer. "Don't put me in this position," he said.

"What's the matter?" Kiezlow said. "An hour ago you wanted to drive to Canada. You wanted to live out of the truck."

"Yeah, but we could get arrested for this."

"What, do you think you can't get arrested for stealing a truck?"

"I was just kidding," Schneider said. It was obvious, he thought.

"What?"

"I was just kidding," Schneider said, almost shouting. His eyes felt hot; tears had formed behind them, and he kept his eyes focused on Kiezlow so as not to let the tears out.

Kiezlow was looking into the distance, over Schneider's shoulder, with a private, melancholy expression. Then, abruptly, he started back around the truck for the driver's side.

"I just wanted to hear you say it," he said, and climbed back into the cab.

MOMENT

H e walked around back of the movie theater in the glaring heat, carrying a brown bag with a small carton of lemonade in it. The digital temperature on the Jackson Building had said ninety-seven degrees. He was so thirsty after only having crossed Main Street and walked along the half-block length of the theater that he couldn't believe it. It was too hot outside, but he didn't want to stay in the waiting room anymore. They said it would take another half hour, and he came out to get away from it.

He sat down on the cracked sidewalk behind the theater, although it offered no shade. It was a place to be away from everything. He pulled the lemonade out of the bag. Weeds stuck up out of the cracks in the cement around him, and pieces of broken bottles were scattered around. Two parked cars sat in the big parking lot, pointed in different directions; across the lot, the elevated platform for the railroad shone bright gray in the midday sun. He drank some of the lemonade. He could tell right away that it wouldn't take care of his thirst; he would want more as soon as it was finished.

When he and Nina were first going out, she used to come to his place dressed in a jumper and sit on the red folding chair with one of her legs straight out and one bent back under, watching him. She had just gotten out of high school, and the ten-year age difference was exciting to both of them. They made love for hours at a time. He brought in ice cream and they sat Indian-style, naked on the bed, and ate it out of the same bowl. He remembered her laughing at things he said, but he couldn't remember what they were. He had been able to make her laugh without thinking about it.

It would be so easy to start walking across the parking lot with the asphalt hot under his thin sneaker soles, kicking a pebble out of his way and passing close by the bumper of the car nearest him, with its blue paint job almost translucent in the vicious sun, crossing the service road and entering the shade under the train platform and walking up the concrete stairs with the metal railing cool on his hand, coming out up on top with a breeze up there and looking out over the Concord Dry Cleaner and the supermarket that used to be Bohack's and the alley with the big garbage bins, and finally the next train pulling in, steel-gray, blurred, loud, blocking the view, slowing to a stop, the doors hissing open and the air conditioning spilling out. But he didn't want to be closed in.

It would have been better to have the keys to one of the cars. He could open the door with the chrome handle that glinted in the sun, roll down the window, then slide in under the wheel with the car seat hot on his legs through his jeans and the air hot and close around his head, lean over and roll down the window on the passenger side, then turn the key in the ignition and feel the car start up, slide her into drive, wheel her around sharp and out of the parking lot and down the road with the wind whipping in the windows and that exhilaration of being able to go anywhere. He would have paid anything to feel that again.

He picked up a large pebble and held it in the palm of his hand. He stared at it. It had weight; it existed. Then he threw it out into the parking lot and it hit the asphalt dully, skidding and rolling along and finally stopping. The day was still the same. Throwing the rock had been an exertion, and suddenly he felt alone.

His head was heavy. He needed to get out of the sun. It was getting close to the time anyway. Thoughts entered his mind one at a time, like characters walking onto an empty stage, reading a line and then leaving. He drank off the rest of the lemonade, then he stood up and started back around the theater toward Main Street. He thought he might go back to the deli and get some club soda, but he knew it would be better to just head back to the air-conditioned waiting room.

At the Medical Building he took the elevator to the second floor, where a muted bell announced his entrance. The nurse at the desk looked up at him, then back down without greeting him. It was so cool in there. He was self-conscious again about his T-shirt and paint-splattered work jeans. Before he sat down, he went to get a drink at the water fountain. Inside the stainless steel fountain, set into the wall, was a sign reading IMPORTANT: *Do not drink any fluids for five hours before the procedure.*

Four women were waiting, paging through magazines or staring absently at nothing. One had a young girl with her, which surprised him. The low hum of distant machinery emanated from behind the wood-paneled walls, as if they were deep in the hold of a huge boat. On the low white end table next to his seat, he pushed aside a few copies of *Prevention* magazine, located a copy of *Time,* and looked through it at the pictures.

Not long afterward, a door opened at the opposite end of the room from the nurse's desk, and Nina walked out, smiling vaguely and walking deliberately, as if she had just stepped off a boat onto a dock. He stood up and walked over as soon as he saw her.

"Hi, Boo," she said, a little sleepily. She let him kiss her on the cheek.

"How are you? Are you okay?"

"I'm fine. It's good to see you. Let's go home."

"I'll go get the car," he said. She was shivering a little; she had worn only that T-shirt and a pair of shorts. He was relieved that she looked the same as she had before.

"That's okay," she said. "I want to walk a little."

"Do you know how hot it is out there?"

"I don't care, Boo, I just want to walk." She wasn't smiling, and he realized she was probably stressed out.

"Okay," he said. "Okay. Come on. Let's go." He put his arm around her, and they walked toward the door. She had filled out the card and forms beforehand, so they could just leave. Nobody looked up at them as they walked out into the afternoon. Maybe he could take her for a soda or something. It was hard to know, these days, what would cheer her up.

Port Isabel Hurricane

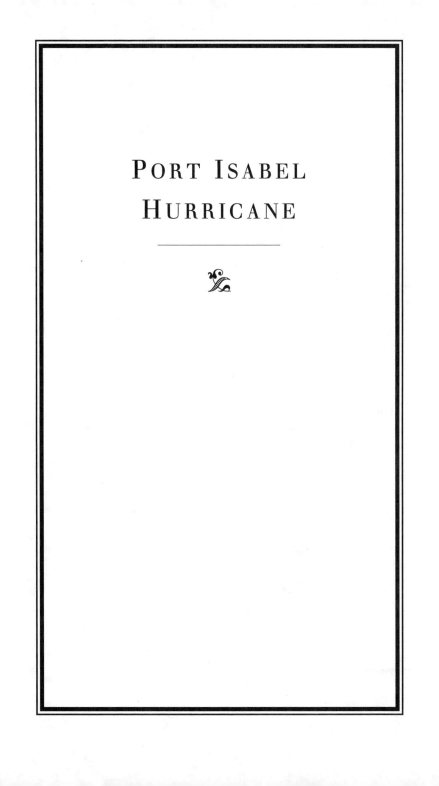

The rain had started the night before. At first it blew against the windows of Hector Flores's house in tentative gusts, making a spattering noise as if someone were flinging handfuls of dry rice at the panes. The wind picked up steadily as the night went on, and now it drove the rain before it in torrents under the bruised morning sky. News broadcasts predicted that the hurricane, if it struck with full force, would leave tens of thousands homeless along Texas's southern coast.

Hector Flores slid an unframed mirror from under the drainboard in his bathroom, pulled a small vial from his pocket and laid out two lines of cocaine on the glass. His wife, Jodi, was getting their daughter ready, and Jodi's *abuelita,* her mother's mother, was in the kitchen, putting food into shopping bags. They were a half hour late getting out; the citizens of Port Isabel had been ordered to evacuate by eight A.M. to the high school in Los Fresnos, the same one where Jodi taught gym. There was nothing left for Hector to do. His boat was in Horacio's warehouse over by Laguna Vista, and all the floating docks had been stowed under the north deck at Dan's Pier. The county had turned off the electricity and water out on South Padre to make sure nobody stayed there. Hector was surprised that Port Isabel still had power.

As he bent to the mirror to inhale the lines, his face loomed up before him, disembodied, the Mexican Indian features tinted the color of tomato paste from fishing the south Texas coast, his eyes circled by two pink rings where his sunglasses had made permanent shadows. He looked into the eyes as if they belonged to an unfamiliar and potentially threatening stranger, deep brown and slightly bloodshot, then the nose with its enlarged pores, the tiny hairs coming out of the nostrils, then, pulling back his lips, his teeth, which seemed sound and white. A film of sweat had broken out on his face. He inhaled the lines; the cocaine burned in the back of his nose like a welder's arc. For a moment, he imagined that he was burning himself from the inside out for heat and light.

Hector Flores was the best and the best-known fishing guide in the area. He had grown up without shoes not far from the neighborhood where he now owned the most substantial house, a three-bedroom ranch made of cinderblocks. Wealthy Anglos paid him large sums to take them around Laguna Madre in his shallow-draft boat with his name stenciled in blue script along the side. He was both envied and admired by the others whose families had come over from

Mexico at the same time his had, and whom he thought of disparagingly as *mojados,* or wetbacks.

Like most people in the lower Rio Grande Valley, Hector took nothing for granted. Yet in the past weeks he had fallen prey to something he could not explain, a fantasy of leaving his life behind. It had started two months earlier, around the time he met Debra Soffer, an assistant professor at the community college in Harlingen, and the feeling puzzled him even as he found himself increasingly occupied by it.

When this storm began moving toward the Texas coast, the feeling had become more disturbing to him, more acute. The harder he tried to fight it, the more compelling it became. Perhaps in compensation, he had grown obsessive about details in preparing for the storm—not just boarding windows and securing the backyard furniture, but wrapping everything of value in plastic or blankets and stashing it in a closet or drawer. If the storm were as bad as they said it would be, none of his efforts would make any difference. Yet he had spent the day before in manic preparation—all the while half wishing for the entire slate to be washed clean. With nothing left to do now, he was like an engine revving faster and faster with no load on it. The only thing he thought would satisfy him was talking to Debra, which he couldn't do until he got to the high school. He wiped the mirror with a fingertip and went out to see if everything was ready.

Hector walked past the hall closet, where his fishing trophies, usually displayed in the living room, were wrapped in plastic and stored on the top shelf, along with the mounted snook with which he had taken first prize at age twelve in the junior Laguna Madre tournament. Gifts given him by some of his wealthy clients were packed into the bedroom closet, also wrapped in plastic—a silver serving bowl engraved with his name, an autographed photo of the Penthouse Pet of the Year that he got when the Marstons took him and Jodi to Las Vegas, a china platter shaped like a bonito. The CD system, the tape deck, and the VCR were packed and stowed in the den closet.

In the den he found his seven-year-old, Linda, sitting on the floor watching the color television; it was expensive, with a walnut cabinet, and Hector had placed it up on boards on the couch. Terrible pictures from the Caribbean flashed across the screen—houses destroyed by fallen trees, cars stuck in knee-deep mud, people crowded into refugee tents. Outside the sliding glass doors to the backyard, it was as dark as the half hour before nightfall.

"Where's Mommy?" Hector asked her. She stared at the television, her cheeks wet with tears. She had inherited all his Indian features rather than the smoother, lighter ones from the Anglo side of Jodi's family; she looked, in fact, like the only picture Hector had seen of his own mother when she was young.

"Hey," he said, "hey—Daddy's going to take care of you. You know that, right? Nothing is going to happen." Hector turned the television off, saying, "Those pictures are from somewhere else. We're going to the school until this passes, then we'll come home and everything will be fine." He could feel the cocaine coming on.

He bent down to her. "Don't be scared, sweetheart," he said, stroking her hair. The wind lashed the trees in the backyard.

"Will you and Mommy stay with me if the storm blows our house down?" she asked.

Hector stopped stroking her hair. He looked into her deep brown eyes and for a moment was aware of a powerful sense that she was making fun of him, or that she had discovered his affair with Debra and was baiting him. As quickly as it came, the feeling was gone, replaced by an almost complete incomprehension of the question.

"Why do you ask a question like that?" he said. "Nothing is going to happen. No one is going anywhere."

Route 100 was empty all the way to Los Fresnos. The rain came down in gusting, slanting sheets and the wind blew the traffic lights almost horizontal on their wires at the intersections. Jodi sat next to Hector in front, singing songs over the back of the seat to Linda, while her *abuelita* clapped her hands in an effort to divert the child. The wind was trying to steer the car off the road, and Hector drove with a furious concentration; when they were five minutes from the school, he snapped at them all to be quiet.

He was relieved to pull into the high school parking lot, where cars had parked in tight double rows along the side, and then, finally, all over—on the lawn and even on the sidewalks. Hector pulled up as near to the main entrance as he could, parked, and then walked evenly in the rain while his family ran ahead of him into the building, where they were directed to the gymnasium.

The gym was full of people from all the surrounding communities—Mexicans, Anglos, older-stock *Tejanos* of Mexican ancestry; the bleachers had been pulled out and people had spread sleeping bags under the bright lights on the varnished basketball court; the Mexicans sat in beach chairs and folding chairs around coolers full of food, talking loudly and listening for news of the hurricane's progress on their radios. From the far end of the gymnasium the hollow thunk of bouncing basketballs punctuated the unmuffled din of voices echoing off the sky-blue cinderblock walls. Grandparents shepherded renegade kids, and parents stood around gossiping with the teachers as if they were at open house. The atmosphere was almost festive, even though everyone could have been close to losing everything they had. Disaster had liberated them, for a while, from routine.

As they walked in, Hector felt himself disappearing under the bright, shadowless lights, and he put his sunglasses on. The translucent panels along the tops of the gym walls were as dark as during a night basketball game, and even over the noise in the gym Hector could hear them groaning with the wind. He led his three women toward an empty section of the bleachers, away from people, without looking left or right. Jodi waved to Carla, another gym teacher, across the basketball court. Hector ignored the exchange; he felt as uncomfortable around the teachers who worked with his wife as he did around the lower-class Mexicans with their tacos and hair pomade.

"Hector," Jodi said, "I think I forgot the bottle opener."

"What do we need it for?" he said. "Borrow one from somebody."

They put their bags down in front of the bleachers and Jodi helped Linda off with her raincoat. Carla walked over, greeted Hector respectfully, then began talking to Jodi. Soon afterward, Hector told Jodi he needed to call Scotty, one of the other guides at Dan's Pier, and walked off across the gym.

Hector found a phone booth at the other end of the school, in the lobby outside the auditorium, and called Debra's number in McAllen. The lobby was dark; outside the windows the wind and rain flayed the trees. He felt as if he were somewhere far out at sea, calling shore. He pictured Debra lying in bed in a light cotton flannel nightgown, with her brown hair feathered across one cheek. The phone picked up.

"Hello," her voice said, distracted sounding, tense.

"It's me," Hector said, quietly.

"Hector?" she said, focusing. "Where are you?"

"We're at the high school. We got here about ten minutes ago."

"The lights just went off," she said. "I'm a little scared."

"You don't have to be scared; your building is solid. Besides, you're too far inland for flooding, and up on the hill."

"I know," she said. "But I've never seen weather like this. I mean, don't worry; I have candles and everything. Are you okay?"

"Yeah," he said, "I'm okay." Hector felt good hearing her voice; it was warm and breathy, not weighed down and preoccupied, or strident, like Jodi's could be. "Hey—I read that book, the letters from the poet."

"Did you like it?"

"Yeah. He was very, uh, alone. Both of them were alone." Outside the windows, a giant cardboard carton blew in the rain end over end across the mud-green lawn and the charcoal sky.

When Hector was young, he had told her once, his father made fun of him for reading. His father worked in the canneries and was very sarcastic and discouraging about anything that involved Anglo culture. Hector had left school after seventh grade, but he was smart, he was curious. When he met Debra, at a bar on South Padre called Great Expectations, he was immediately intrigued that she was a teacher. She had been in the area for only a month and a half. She and two other teachers from the college were drinking at a table, celebrating one of their birthdays. He was there to meet a fishing client from Albuquerque, who was late, and one of Debra's friends had started talking to him, coming on to him. But it was Debra he had noticed; she was quieter, with eyes that took everything in. Her hair was back in a bun and she had what looked like a chopstick stuck through it, and she looked at him shyly, although she had been laughing and talking with the other two before he came over. He had noticed her before they started talking to him. The others were dressed like they were trying to pick some-one up. He sat down at their table and asked them where they taught. The other two were from the valley; one was Mexican and one was Anglo, brassy Anglo, a sorority girl from a state university.

"What do you teach?" he asked the one he liked, whose name was Debra.

"Comparative literature," she said.

"What do you compare it to?" he asked.

The sorority sister laughed. Her whiskey sour glass sat empty in front of her. "You're funny," she said.

"I teach French and Russian literature together," Debra said.

"Like Tolstoy?" he said. *"War and Peace?"*

"I don't teach that book, but I teach some Tolstoy," she said. "Have you read much of him?" she said, without any of the condescension he might have expected.

"Uh, 'The Master and the Man,' " he said. He had read it in an old, coverless short-story collection he had found in his uncle's house in San Antonio.

Before he left the table to meet his client, he knew her full name and where she taught, and he called her at the Comp Lit department the next day. She wasn't there, and he left his number at Dan's Pier for her to call, and she did call, later the same day. She came down and he took her out in the bay in the brilliant August sunshine, and that was the start of that.

He had never been able to talk to anyone before about his private feelings, or about books. Fishing, he had told her, was the only acceptable way for him to be alone and think when he was growing up. She seemed interested in everything he said, and she seemed to understand his loneliness. To him, it felt was as if he were seeing himself in a mirror for the first time. And it had made him feel, consciously, that something had been missing in his life.

"Hector," Debra said now, on the telephone, "only you could discuss Rilke in the middle of a hurricane evacuation."

"I don't like to sit around and talk about nothing," he said, "or about what I bought at the Kmart." This was all anyone talked about, he thought. Except for the guides, good fishing talk sometimes. Sometimes a little more. "What are you going to do until it blows over?"

"I don't know. I probably have enough candles to read. I don't know if I could concentrate."

"Yeah," he said. He tried to imagine her there, what the apartment would look like in candlelight, with all the books and the big poster from the Italian art exhibit in Boston. He closed his eyes and thought about being there with her reading to him. He liked to ask her about Boston, where she was from. She had said that lots of people fished up there, but she had never gone fishing. He had never been to that part of the country, he had said, so they were even. She had shown him a copy of *Moby Dick*, with great woodcut pictures of the whale boats, with their high bows so unlike the flat ones they used fishing the bay.

"How are Jodi and Linda doing?"

Hector looked across the darkened lobby; against the far wall stood two barely discernible potted palms. It startled him to hear their names in Debra's voice. It was unpleasant, like being awakened by a policeman.

"They're fine," he said.

"Is Linda scared?"

"There's nothing to be scared about."

Debra was quiet for a second, then she said, "Hector, is something wrong?"

"Nothing's wrong."

"Okay."

"Everything's fine, and everybody's fine."

"What's it like at the school?"

"It's like a party."

"Hector," she said, "what's wrong?"

"Nothing. Why do you think something's wrong?"

"You sound angry."

"I'm not angry. Everybody's in the gym, and all the wetbacks are sitting around like they're at a barbecue."

They were quiet, again, for a moment. "Is everything packed up all right in your house?" Debra said.

"Sure," Hector said. He kept her separate from his everyday life, and it was angering him to be asked about that life now. "Listen," he said, "I don't care if the house blows down."

"Hector," Debra said, "what are you talking about?"

"What?"

"What do you mean you don't care?"

"I can make a living either way. I can fish anywhere."

"I don't understand why you're saying this," Debra said. "Everything that means anything to you is in that house. You shouldn't say things like that."

"Hey," he said, "what will be will be, you know? I don't have a crystal ball to look in."

"I . . . I know. I guess I'm not sure why you're saying this. You must be upset. I wish I could see you."

"I'm not upset," he said. "Hey, I've seen hurricanes before."

Debra was quiet, and Hector looked around the darkened lobby and felt suddenly strange, spooked, as if ghosts were hiding in the shadows. It was quiet except for the rain outside and the system noise on the phone in his ear.

"Say something," he said.

"I'm not sure what to say," she said. "You don't sound like yourself."

"Right," he said. He thought he saw movement across the lobby, but his eyes were playing tricks on him. He tried to imagine being out on the bay, in the sharp focus of high afternoon. "Hey, Debra," he said, "I've got to go. After this is over I'm going to take you out fishing, okay?"

"Okay."

"Are you okay or what?"

"I'm okay. I just, I don't know. You sound so . . . detached suddenly."

"Hey, don't worry," he said. "I'm fine. You'll be fine. Don't worry about anything."

"All right."

"Okay. I'll check you later."

When he got off the phone he left the booth and walked quickly across the lobby, looking straight ahead. I'll take her out past Punta Gorda, he thought. We can pack a lunch and eat in the cove.

The fluorescent lamps in the men's room gave a good, shadowless light. Hector laid out four more lines on the metal ledge under the mirrors. Joker watched him, his face red and puffy, with sandy, curly hair blown all over. He wore a T-shirt, ragged denim shorts, and sneakers; the front of the left sneaker had been torn off and a bandaged foot stuck out. The week before, he had cut off his big toe mowing Hector's lawn.

Hector felt good in the bathroom; it was like a bunker in one of the World War II movies he liked to watch as a kid. He felt in control of the visible reality. The luminous sense that he was in control was almost too good to support. As he chopped the coke down with a razor, Hector told Joker a story about the wife of one of his clients; her husband had gone off for the afternoon with another guide from Dan's, and she had Hector up in Saida Towers for the afternoon serving him champagne in bed. As Hector told the story he could feel the admiration, the wonder, and the hunger that it made in Joker's mind. He sensed Joker getting greedier and more dependent, and it made Hector start laughing as he told Joker about how the woman and her husband came down to the pier the next day, and the husband strutted around acting the seasoned fisherman; Joker laughed along with Hector, but they were laughing about different things, and that made Hector laugh even more, and he started laughing so hard he had to put the razor down. When he was able to look at Joker again, he saw a trusting face, a little scared. Hector shook his head slightly and arranged the coke into lines again with the razor.

"Hey," Hector said, "how's your foot, man?"

"It hurts sometime, you know, but it's okay."

"When the doctor said the bandage could come off?" He pulled a new twenty-dollar bill from his billfold, rolled it tight, and handed it to Joker. He was feeling badly about laughing at him.

Joker took the bill, inhaled two lines, and said, "The doctor said two weeks. Every night I have to change it anyway. It's ugly, man, all black and shit."

Hector did the other two lines. The weekend before they had had a cookout at his house with all the guys, and he had cooked up some venison that his cousin had killed, venison and redfish on either side of the grill, and Joker hadn't wanted to eat the venison, saying, "I don't want to eat Bambi, man. It spooks me thinking about the way a deer looks at you and shit," and everybody had made fun of him. Hector had said, "Hey, you think a cow doesn't look you in the eye? How come you eat a steak and you don't eat a deer?" And Noey had said, "Joker never saw the front end of a cow; he always comes up behind them." That had been some funny shit. Afterward they went inside and Hector showed them the *Great Heavyweights* video and they all sat

around drinking Heinekens. It was the same thing he remembered from when he was a kid, the men talking and joking roughly. Except everybody lived doubled up in houses,
uncles and aunts, a whole different thing, one or two cars
they all had to share. He had never liked being around his
father and his friends; it was better to be alone, and it was
strange to him that his skill on the water, his loneliness and
intuition, had only led him to a place where he had all these
other people around, talking the same shit with them, giving them work. He thought about being out on the bay the
last time with his Anglo friend Bob from *Southern Fisheries*
magazine; they had gone out for shark, just for kicks, and
Bob had caught two snook with the shark rig. Come up to
San Antonio, Bob had said, proud of himself, joking. I catch
marlin right there in the river all the time. I'll get you a job
cooking at Lucinda's; you could learn a lot from me. Hector had laughed, but the remark had ruined the friendship
for him. What, he thought, did Bob know about having to
cook for three dollars an hour and bring the money home to
feed everybody else? Hector would never go back to something like that; he had spent too much time growing up with
it. The thought caused an unaccountable feeling of panic to
collect in him, like a sudden bruise spreading right in the
middle of his chest, around where the cocaine was making
his heart thrum like an engine.

Hector looked around the bathroom; Joker stood with his
hands in his pockets. The bright shadowless light on the
gray glazed cinderblocks was spooking him as much as the

lobby had spooked him before. "Hey," he said, surprised to hear his voice sounding so familiar, "I'm sorry I said that thing about the deer, man."

Joker watched him with a tentative smile, as if he were waiting for Hector's comment to crystallize into some joke. When nothing more came, Joker said, "What deer?"

Back in the gym, the tone and pace of things had changed. It seemed less densely populated; the basketball had more or less stopped; only a few of the younger kids ran around at the far end.

Hector saw Jodi waving to him as he walked in. When he walked over, she told him that the storm had blown sharply north and was now expected to strike land just above Galveston. Bad as it had seemed, the storm had only grazed the Port Isabel area. The radio had said they were expecting substantial problems in places, but nothing like the wholesale catastrophe they had predicted. There were no details on their area yet, so they could have no idea what had happened to their house. But the worst of the storm was over for them, and Galveston and Port Arthur were now bracing for landfall.

Hector was quiet for a moment, then he said, "Come on; let's go back."

"Do you think it's all right to leave?" Around them, people were folding up their chairs and gathering their things; many of them avoided each other's eyes, some moved slowly as if in no hurry to find out whatever bad news awaited them, others gave terse orders to children and wives, a very few men joked among themselves with fatalistic bravura.

"The storm isn't coming here," Hector said, "so it's all right."

They got their things assembled and headed out of the gym in the midst of the general exodus. Outside the school, the sky had already started clearing. Patches of blue showed through the disintegrating gray clouds. They had been at the high school for less than three hours. The speed with which the storm was dispersing was almost as terrible as its intensity while it lasted.

Hector was silent all the way back to Port Isabel. Cars had emerged onto the roads like insects. Sometimes he had to slow his car to a crawl to negotiate ponds of water that straddled the roads at low points. As they passed Lee's department store, Jodi pointed out a huge tree on its side in the parking lot. For the most part, however, the destruction they saw seemed only cosmetic.

By the time they turned onto their street, fifteen minutes later, the sun shone on everything with a painful clarity. Shimmering droplets of water dripped from silent tree branches. The sun was warm and brilliant and the street had already started drying. One tree had blown down. The house itself seemed fine—the roof on, the window boards intact. Some of the flowers in the front bed had been torn out, and the garbage cans were over by the fence. Hector went to get them. Jodi approached the front door with her grandmother and Linda tentatively, as if all the damage might be hidden inside.

"Come on," Hector said impatiently, walking past them, getting out his own keys. "What do you expect—that something is going to jump out at you? Everything is fine." He unlocked the door, pushed it open and walked in ahead of them. "Nothing happened," he said. "What are you waiting for?"

Inside the darkened house, everything stood as they had left it.

"You see?" Hector said. "Nothing's different. What's the matter? Here, look." He grabbed Jodi by the wrist and pulled her to the den, where the television rested securely on the boards he had placed across the couch.

"Hector, you're hurting me."

Jodi pulled her arm away, then she left the room and went to the kitchen. Her *abuelita* still stood by the front door, hands clasped in prayer, talking in Spanish to her God. Linda stood in the middle of the living room crying. Hector came out from the den and saw her.

"Hey," Hector said, "what's wrong?"

His daughter kept crying, standing in the middle of the floor with her eyes closed.

"Hey," he said, looking down at her. "Do you hear?"

She looked up at him, still crying, unable to answer, and he grabbed her by one shoulder and shook her. "Answer me," he said. "What's wrong? Everything's fine. Nothing happened." She began crying harder, and Hector felt anger welling up at his inability to make her realize that things were all right. He shook her again. "What are you crying about?" he yelled, but she only stood there, her pink face contorted in anguish, unanswering and unreachable.

Burn Me Up

F uck you. Fuck you. Stay the fuck out of my dressing room. I'm not the fucking janitor here, and I don't want you the fuck in my dressing room." Billy Sundown stopped hollering at the club owner for a moment as he opened the door to his dressing room and saw his younger sister, a middle-aged woman in a pink blazer that was too tight on her, sitting in a folding chair. "Hey, Georgia," Billy said. "How you doin'? You need anything?"

"Hi, Billy," she said.

"No, man," Billy started up again, turning to find the club owner still there, "I'm not foolin' with you, son. I'm not too old to cut you a new asshole. And why wasn't the piano tuned, as is *stipulated*"—he paused on the word, for effect— "in my contract?"

The club owner, whose father had been in grade school with Billy, stood there, looking at Billy's Adam's apple, unsure what to say. Billy watched him for a second and shook his head pityingly. "Come in here, son," Billy said suddenly. "You look like you need a drink. You look like you're gonna pass out. Come on in. Give us your tired, your weary . . ."

He held the door open and the club owner, a pale, nervous man of thirty-four with a receding hairline and a half-hearted mustache, walked into the small, cramped room, nodded to Billy's sister, and sat down next to some stacked-up beer cases, wiping his forehead with a handkerchief. It was springtime in Memphis, but inside the Alamo Show Bar it was always some indeterminate season of extremes, with hot, torpid air smelling of beer and sweat suddenly giving way to blasts of freezing air from the overworked air-conditioning system.

"Now, what do you need to talk to me about, son?" Billy said, pouring bourbon into a small, pleated paper cup. "Why don't you put some goddamn glasses in the dressing rooms, too. This Wild Turkey'll burn a hole right through these things. How was that first set, Jo-jo?" He began stripping off his bright green shirt; perspiration had soaked through the tuxedo-shirt ruffles that ran down the front.

His sister smiled at the pet nickname and said, "Great. Ron wanted to know if you'd play 'Burn Me Up' in the next set."

"Anything any husband of any sister of mine wants he gets, as long as it's not a loan. I been broke too goddamn long." He looked at the club owner again, as if he had just appeared out of nowhere. "What the fuck do you want? I thought I told you to get out of here."

"We should probably talk about it in private," the club owner said, wincing as he watched Billy down the bourbon.

"Anything you got to say to me you can say in front of my own flesh and blood." Billy peeled off his undershirt, picked a towel off the top of the stack of beer cases, and began toweling himself off.

"So be it," the young man said. "Several of the customers complained about the language you used onstage, and the man you threw the wet napkin at is a city councilman."

Billy looked at him in stunned amazement. "A city councilman? You mean Lucas?"

"Yes, I mean Mr. Lucas."

"Look, son. I went to junior high school with that pencil dick. I remember when he used to try and keep his girlfriends away from me. Fuck him." He looked over at his sister and began to laugh. She raised her eyebrows noncommittally and opened her purse, looking in it for something. "Well, what do you want me to do, get his suit dry-cleaned for him?"

"I want you to apologize. You embarrassed the man in front of his wife and two guests that he brought to hear you play."

"Hear me play? Am I doing that peckerwood some kinda favor by playing here? He used to keep away from me like you'd keep away from a goddamn copperhead. Now he wants to show all his friends he's a pal of Billy Sundown's, then they talk through the middle of when I'm playing—"

"You don't understand—"

"Don't tell me I don't understand shit. Since when did

city councilmen come to see rock and roll? I remember when they tried to run me out for playin' it. Now I'm rediscovered and it's a big gravy train for everybody. What do you need, Jo-jo? You're making me nervous."

"I was just looking for my lipstick."

"Son, why don't you be a good boy and go back to the sound booth and tell them to bring the mike up a little more on the bass, and leave me alone."

"Look, Billy, everybody loves to hear you perform—"

"I know it."

"—and I do, too."

"Fine. Your daddy used to help me set up equipment."

"I know that." The younger man looked at the floor between his feet for a moment; he was suddenly very tired. "Would you please do me a favor and just go out and apologize to Mr. Lucas? It would help me out, believe me."

Billy scratched his head; the red hair so prominent in the history-of-rock books and retrospective television specials was dyed now to cover the gray. "What is your poppa doing now, anyway?" he asked the young man.

"He still owns the dealership out on North Parkway."

"That's good," Billy said, thoughtfully. "All right, let me visit with my sister a little bit here."

"Please," the young man said, "go out to see Mr. Lucas before your next—"

"Goddamn it anyway, son," Billy said, "I told you I would, now quit crawling up my asshole."

"Okay," the younger man said. He couldn't remember Billy agreeing to do it, but he decided not to make an issue of it. "I'm sorry. Fine. Thanks." He left the room, closing the door soundlessly behind him.

"That fella just ain't in the right business," Billy said, shaking his head.

"You talked pretty rough to him."

"I know it," he said, pulling on a fresh shirt. "Me and his daddy used to be friends. Maybe I'll go out and say something to Lucas in a bit. Maybe I won't. City councilman . . . Christ on a Harley. You sure you don't want something to drink? They put some Cokes in the little fridge."

"I'm fine," she said, looking up at her brother through her bifocals and smiling.

This was the second time Billy had played at the Alamo Show Bar since the resurgence of interest in 1950s rock and roll that had led to his rediscovery. The Alamo was a roadhouse just northeast of downtown Memphis, a giant, barnlike room with pool tables and pinball machines at the far end and a parquet dance floor around which tables were arranged, the kind of place that featured small acts on their way to the top and big acts on their way to the bottom. And sometimes it featured someone like Billy, a big act that had hit bottom and bounced back up to the middle.

In the late 1950s, he had been one of the original Wild Men of Rock and Roll. Film footage from that time shows him standing on the piano, throwing his head back, playing bare-chested. One columnist called him the "Redneck Rachmaninoff." Big package tours, lots of money, leopard-print Cadillacs. Then, while Billy was on tour in Ohio, an enterprising reporter discovered that Billy's female traveling companion of the moment was only sixteen years old, and a resident of Kentucky to boot. That Billy had transported a minor across state lines made all the newspapers; he narrowly escaped imprisonment for violating the Mann Act, his first wife divorced him, and by that time—1960— his brand of rock and roll was being eclipsed in favor of milder teen idols like Pat Boone and Frankie Avalon. Billy's career went into a long slide.

For most of the ensuing three decades, he ground out a living playing in dismal bars and lounges, living on hamburgers and Dexedrine, driving alone to Holiday Inns in Biloxi, Mississippi, or Carbondale, Illinois, playing on a portable electric piano with a local drummer. A small sign in the lobby, maybe—TONIGHT ONLY—BILLY SUNDOWN— with one or two of his hit song titles listed under it to jog people's memories. Drunken salesmen would sing along with him as he did perfunctory versions of his own hits and standard rock and roll covers like "Blue Suede Shoes" and "Great Balls of Fire." About midway through any given evening, the bourbon and speed that he liked to mix would kick in, and Billy would abandon his set pattern and begin playing boogie woogie versions of obscure tunes he remembered from childhood, like "Shadow in the Pines" and "The Girl with the Blue Velvet Band." He was famous for getting into fights, and his reputation was not good.

In the mid-1970s, he underwent a supposed religious conversion. He had his own evangelical television show for a while in Los Angeles, on which he played piano and sang songs like "I'll Fly Away" and "Walk and Talk with Jesus" with a beat that some felt was not conducive to a prayerful attitude. Every month he sent home as much as he could to his mother, sometimes as little as thirty dollars after dry-cleaning bills and alimony payments to his first and second wives. Eventually he got into a mess over the wife of one of the television station executives, and he went back to the rounds of Holiday Inn lounges.

After about twenty-five years, nostalgic pieces about early rock and roll began to appear in magazines. Several television specials were produced; it was far enough behind, safe enough, to have become a period piece. Billy Sundown, certainly one of the best-known figures of the time, a real outlaw, was prominent in all of them. Promoters hunted him up, helped him put together a band; he played a series of big arenas, often in package shows teaming him with other legends like Chuck Berry and Fats Domino. He headlined large, hip rock clubs in major cities. His old recordings were packaged into new boxed sets with attractive graphics.

Billy Sundown didn't seem to have changed at all, except for a slight paunch and the obviously dyed hair. He would still do anything to get to a sluggish crowd—bang the piano cover against the piano's body, throw things, stand on the keys. The promoters made money off of him, but he was trouble. Billy felt not so much grateful for as vindicated by the revival of his career. He acted as if the fans and the promoters were the ones who had been missing in action for thirty years.

----

*   *   *

Archie Lucas and his party sat at a table just outside the circle of fuchsia and yellow lights from the bandstand and
dance floor, amid all the din of the Alamo. Walter Phillips,
a partner from Archie's old siding business, sat next to
Archie, yelling in his ear.

"Let's get the hell out of here," Walter Phillips said,
sharply, into Archie Lucas's ear. "I know you like his
singing and all, but he's a freak. If we don't leave, *I'm* gonna
punch him out."

"No, you're not, Walter," Phillips's wife said, from across
the table.

"Look, man," Archie said, "I been wanting to hear him
play live for years, and I'm not going to leave now. Besides,
I want to see his expression when I tell him who I am. That's
it, Walter. If you don't want to wait around, that's fine."

"Look," Walter Phillips said, "I got you into this by talking, all right? Whyn't you let me go talk to the manager myself?"

"Whyn't you have another drink?" Archie took his
glasses off and rubbed his eyes. He pushed inward on the
bridge of his nose with both thumbs and wished that he had
come to see Billy Sundown alone.

With his eyes still closed he thought back to an April day
in 1948. He was in seventh grade, the first entry class to at-
tend Albert H. Fletcher Junior High School, which had just
opened out east of the city, where they were starting to build
the new neighborhoods for the servicemen who had made

it back from the war. The new school pulled in kids from the nearby neighborhoods, as well as some from farther away; children from solid middle-class families like Archie's sat in scrubbed new classrooms next to the ragged children of factory hands and truck drivers and cotton exchange strongbacks. Archie's father owned a liquor store downtown; his older brother had been killed in the Pacific, two months before V-J Day. He and his parents had moved to a new house in a subdivision that winter, in the middle of the school year, a gray, dislocating time. The houses there were small and identical, and they sat on small, treeless plots on tracts of land that had been farmland before the war.

Spring came; the sun bore down on the shadowless sidewalks and fledgling lawns. The days were getting longer. Every week Archie went with his parents to the outdoor concerts in Overton Park, and sat under the sky with its early moon and listened to light opera, or whatever they were offering. Some essential tension that had been in the air for as long as he could remember had dissipated. Archie would always mark that spring as the beginning of a new feeling in himself that he couldn't quite identify, a sense of longing and possibility mixed with a strange directionlessness. The war had given his entire early childhood a direction, a valence. Things were important; letters arrived from far away. Now there was just an odd sense of reality spreading out around him, getting thinner and thinner, like a drop of oil on water.

One day, after school had let out for the afternoon, the new feeling came over Archie suddenly, and especially powerfully. Everything around him seemed new, yet timeless and static at the same time. The warm air, the patches of weeds here and there, the sunlight on the beige bricks of the school building, all seemed oddly palpable, full of meaning. He decided to walk the mile back to his house. He began walking across the school grounds, past the blacktop playground, and started across what would someday be a broad lawn but what was at the time only a field of dirt with a few tufts of weeds sticking up. The top of his head felt hot from the sun.

Suddenly someone appeared in front of him, a skinny kid he had seen in school, one of the older kids, with red hair and a big nose and what looked like a perpetual sneer. White trash, basically, Archie remembered thinking, the kind whose parents lived in the low-income projects along Poplar Avenue. The kid wore a red-and-white striped T-shirt and pants that were a couple of inches too short. He had just appeared, like a vision in the desert. Archie was startled.

"What about you?" the red-haired kid said. His voice had a high, nasal twang to it.

Archie didn't understand the question. "What do you mean 'what about me?' "

The redhead stared at him for a second. "You got any money?"

"No," Archie said. He could hear the drone of an airplane above them in the blue ether, still an unusual sound, but he didn't look up to see it. He kept his eye on the red-haired kid as if he were a snake that had just appeared in his path.

"Lookit this," the redhead said. He held out the palm of

his hand and Archie looked at it. On it sat a light pink, translucent rubber ring, like a miniature trampoline, about an inch and a half across.

"You know what that is?"

"No," Archie said.

"You put that on your John Henry when you do it to a girl."

Across the field in front of the school, Archie saw others walking off toward their homes, in small groups. A circle of sweat had plastered his polo shirt to his belly.

"Cost you a dollar."

"I don't have a dollar for that," Archie said.

"What do you got a dollar for, then?" the redhead said. "You got a dollar to keep me from kicking the shit out of you?"

Archie just stood looking at the redhead. He didn't say anything. The redhead was watching him.

"You like it here?" the redhead said.

"Where?"

The redhead shook his head, looked across the playground. He bent over and picked up a rock from the scrubby ground. "You dress like you got money," he said. "I mean don't you want to get out of here?"

"Out of school?" Archie said.

The redhead squinted at him. Archie looked at his big ears; a big dimple sat right in the middle of his narrow chin. "I'm-a buy a whore." After a moment he said, "What's your name?"

"Archie Lucas."

"You're stupider than a rock," the redhead said. He threw the stone he had in his hand off across the hazy playground. "I'm gonna go to California." He walked away.

Archie would always remember the flavor of that encounter, a sense that the red-haired boy couldn't decide whether he wanted to beat him up or be friends with him. He ran into the redhead, who's name was Billy Sindine, several times over the next few years, the last time at a high school dance, while Archie was spooning out some punch for his date. Suddenly Billy appeared next to him, took the ladle when Archie was finished and spooned himself some punch. For a moment they stood side by side, watching the band; Archie's only thought was that Billy might say something to embarrass him in front of his date. Finally, without looking at Archie, Billy said, "That bassist ought to be bagging up groceries down at the Piggly Wiggly." Then Billy was gone, and Archie never heard of him again until 1956; Archie was attending Memphis State and Billy's voice was suddenly coming out of jukeboxes and car radios.

Here was the strange thing: in that piercing, sometimes mocking, sometimes defiant voice, Archie heard something that cut through to the feeling he had the spring he met Billy in the schoolyard. That voice, tremulous and arch one moment, high and nasal and lonesome the next, along with his boogie woogie piano, all run through a heavy echo chamber, somehow expressed both the loneliness and the sense of possibility that he had felt eight years earlier. As Archie ground his way through college and the stages of providing for his family, Billy became a private hero to Archie. He had gotten out of Memphis, seen the world, taken his lumps and stuck by his guns, and Archie admired him for it. For years he had wanted the chance to tell him that, and he had decided that he wasn't leaving tonight before he'd done it.

Billy and Georgia sat nearly knee-to-knee in the tiny dressing room. "How's Mama?" Billy asked his sister. "When'd you start smoking?"

"I been off and on," his sister said, shaking out a match. "She's good. You oughta go out and see her."

"I'm-a get out there tomorrow and visit with her. I'm stayin' up to the Radisson. They got an all-white baby grand piano in the lobby. How's Ron treatin' you?"

"He's fine. He's still out with Federal Express, doing routing. He took me down to Pascagoula for my birthday."

"When was that? How old were you?"

"Month ago. I turned forty-nine. I tell everybody down to the bank I'm thirty-nine, though, just like Jack Benny."

"Jesus ground hog," Billy said. "I got a sister forty-nine years old. You don't look a day over forty-five."

Georgia laughed, exhaling a plume of smoke and stubbing out her cigarette in a plate.

"Luther and Leon are always asking about you," she said.

"Where the hell are my nephews, anyway?"

"They both had to work tonight. Luther's playing in a band."

"In a band?" Billy said. "He's playing that guitar?"

Georgia nodded. "They call the band Alcohol, Tobacco, and Firearms."

"Alcohol, Tobacco, and goddamn Firearms," Billy said, laughing and slamming a beer case with the flat of his hand. "That's what I should call my autobiography."

Georgia laughed, opened her mouth as if to say something, then closed it again without speaking. They were quiet for a moment.

"You know, Billy," she said, picking at a loose thread on her jacket sleeve, "I feel like I'm getting old and I never get to see you anymore. All I catch is a glimpse of you once every year or two."

"More than that and you'd get sick of me quicker'n you could believe."

"Do you still have that place out in California?"

"I pay taxes on it," Billy said, "so I guess I got it." He ran the backs of his fingers under his chin, meditatively, feeling for stubble. "The IRS has got a ring through my nose the size of a Hula Hoop."

"You ever think about getting a home back here, Billy?" she said.

Absently, as if he hadn't heard her, Billy said, "I wish Luther'd stay the hell out of this business."

"You'd be around family," Georgia continued, looking at her brother through her bifocals. "We miss you."

Billy looked up at her now with an appraising look. He could almost, he thought, see the love coming off of her in waves, like heat off a radiator. "You know, Jo," he said, "sooner or later you manage to get around to the same old thing, don't you? I must have told you half a hundred times what I feel about it, but I still hear this. All I ever wanted was to get the hell out of here. Why in the name of Jesus Christ would I want to move back?"

"Billy, please don't get mad."

"This town is a goddamn minimum-security prison. All the gates are wide open, but there's no place to go for a million miles in any direction. These shit heels around here never gave me the time of day. Everybody wanted to kneel on my goddamn nuts. I remember every single one of them dildos. Who the hell ever stayed in Memphis had anyplace better to go?"

Billy looked at his sister, then up at the ceiling. He ran the palm of his hand over his face.

"Look, Jo," he said, "I don't mean it against you. I couldn't be happy anyplace. I got the devil inside me—"

"Billy, I wish you wouldn't say that."

"Well, shit, it's true, ain't it? When have I ever been satisfied with what God gave me? What the fuck did I ever do for anybody?"

"Watch your language around me sometimes, Billy," Georgia said. "You are so . . . prideful. You talk like the Lord has singled you out to suffer."

"I'm not sayin' that—"

"It's a way of setting yourself above others. The Lord gives everyone his own portion, Billy. Everybody has a load to bear."

Billy looked at the floor while she said this. After she finished, he looked up at her, then back down again. He ran his hand through his hair. After a moment he said, "It's hotter'n eight hells in here, isn't it?"

"Billy," his sister began.

"Listen, Jo," he said, "I should get myself together here a little."

"Billy, why don't you come by on Sunday. I'll fix up a dinner."

"That'd be nice," Billy said, standing up. "Tell Ron to get his Ping-Pong table fixed. He still got that thing sitting down in the basement?"

"I think we threw that out a couple of years ago."

"Yeah," Billy said. "Well . . . we can play flip the spoon or something. Give me a kiss. I'll see you on Sunday not too early."

Georgia gave her brother a kiss and a hug. As she left the dressing room he was fitting cufflinks into his shirt cuffs.

After the door closed, Billy reached into a small briefcase on his dressing table. He hummed softly, "She got a man . . . on her man . . . and a kid man on her kid . . ." He pulled out a tiny plastic bag and opened it.

"Everybody wants to go to heaven," he said to himself, "but nobody wants to die."

From the small bag he pulled out two tiny translucent crystals that looked like rock candy and popped them into his mouth under his tongue. He zipped the bag closed again and stuck it back into the briefcase, which he closed and put on the floor. The crystals dissolved quickly in his mouth, as he buttoned up his shirt. "Sweet to papa," he said, his heart already beating harder.

He tucked his shirt in, breathed deeply. *Love,* he thought, was a word that everybody used, himself included, without knowing what it meant. Some people said God was love. But God was also judgment. They were two sides of the same coin. You get love, but then you have to be worthy of it.

His talent was God-given. But talent can be a judgment on you, too, he thought, just like somebody's love, a gift you didn't ask for. His talent had never seemed like something he owned; it was more like having a brother, a separate part of himself that was better than he was; people loved it and stupidly mistook it for the real him. If they knew what he was really like, they would run away screaming.

He felt the need of some cool water on his face, and he unbuttoned the shirt again and took it off. Jesus loves me, he thought. This I know. Why? 'Cause the Bible tells me so. But I can't sit still for His love. God is love, but love means you have to disappear. If you aren't willing to sacrifice yourself, you can't love. They had been trying to make him disappear without his consent for as long as he could remember. But he wouldn't. Man, he thought, if he wasn't going to hell grits weren't groceries and Mona Lisa was a man.

"I can't sit still . . ." he sang, now, splashing water on his face, making up a song, "for your love, baby." The water refreshed him, pulled him a little bit into focus. He toweled off his face. "I'm doing the multiplication tables of love. Love times five is thirty-five. Love times six is thirty-six . . ." For a second he rested his face in the towel. "Love times seven," he went on, "puts you in heaven. Love times eight turns into hate."

He felt bad about yelling at Georgia. He'd make it up by swallowing his pride in front of Lucas. Just don't let him try and get a piece of me, he thought. Just let me say my piece and get away. How, he wondered, did somebody like Lucas do it? Stay in one place, probably married, kids, a house, friends, cookouts, bowling league, sun comes up, sun goes down, out to dinner once a week when they could get the baby-sitter. Yeah, well, if Lucas has kids, they're probably all grown now. Wonder if he has a daughter . . .

A knock came on the door, and Billy yelled out, "Talk to me."

His bassist, Buzz Clement, opened the door and stuck his head in. "Billy, you want in on a coupla hands of tonk before we got to hit again?"

"Son, I can't take your money like that and get to sleep at night. Besides, I got to go talk to a man out here about something."

Archie Lucas and his party still sat at their table; an embarrassed quiet clung to the group now. Archie tapped a matchbook against the tabletop, rotating it a quarter of a turn for each tap, hitting each edge in turn. His wife, Rose, sat across from him, watching him with a sad look on her face. Walter Phillips and his wife, Rena, were quiet, too. Walter sat to Archie's right, trying to bounce quarters off the table into an empty highball glass.

"Five," Walter Phillips said. "That's five for me. Archie, it's your turn."

"Archie," Rose said. "Why don't we just head out. There's no point—"

"Listen," Archie said, "I want to give it a few minutes, all right? You want to head home, take the car and I'll call a taxi when I'm ready. Please." Archie took his glasses off and began wiping them with a cocktail napkin. The glasses lent his face definition; without them, it was a little unfocused, lined but still boyish, although he was only a year younger than Billy Sundown, and his gray-streaked hair was carefully combed to cover a large bald spot.

"Well, look," Walter Phillips said, pushing his chair back from the table, "we're gonna head home. You sure you're gonna wait around?"

Archie put his glasses back on. "Yeah, I am, in fact."

"Well, I hope you get what you're after," Phillips said, as they walked away.

"Safe home," Archie said.

As his friends walked off through the intermission crowd, Archie tried to formulate in his mind what he would say to Billy when he came out. He could give him an ironic look and say something like, "See if you can guess where we know each other from." Then he could sit there while Billy raked through his mind for the answer. When Billy finally gave up, Archie would remind him of that day on the playground and see if he remembered. Then Archie would tell Billy that he'd been following his career for all these years, and how Billy's recording of "That Lucky Old Sun" had seen him through some tough times. "You made it out of here," he imagined himself saying. "You stuck to your guns." "So did you," he imagined Billy saying. Archie's heart beat harder and he felt a funny tightening in his throat.

As Archie was thinking these thoughts, Billy Sundown emerged from his dressing room and began making his way through the noisy room. He wore a bright purple shirt with tuxedo ruffles down the front, and white pants with white shoes and a yellow belt. As he made his way between the crowded tables he responded to greetings, shook hands, waved, all the while grinding his teeth from the Methedrine he had taken. He made his way straight over to the table where Archie Lucas sat with his wife.

"Howdy, neighbors," Billy said, approaching their table. "Howdy, Mr. Lucas . . . ma'am," nodding to Rose.

Archie felt an adrenaline rush, and an odd, dislocated feeling, too—how had Billy remembered his name after all those years?

"Listen," Billy said, "I wanted to apologize for that incident earlier. Sometimes I get a little jacked up and I forget myself. My apologies to you, too, ma'am."

Archie looked up at Billy Sundown in wonder; the red hair that he remembered from childhood was no longer unkempt, but waved and pomaded into an emblem of controlled wildness. Billy's face looked hollow-cheeked and puffy at the same time. Set into it were a pair of sharp eyes—weird, razorlike eyes like those of old men he'd seen as a boy on trips to visit relatives out in the country, seemingly back-lit by a flame compounded of pure backwoods fanaticism and a strong and uncultivated intelligence. He realized he needed to say something, to acknowledge Billy's apology.

"Well, we shouldn't have been talking while you were playing," Archie said.

"It happens all the time," Billy said, distractedly, his hands in his back pockets. He felt the love waves coming up at him again, just as they did off of Georgia, making him squirm, making him angry. Where, he thought, were all these parasites when he was playing lounges for thirty years? They all wanted something off of him; they wanted him to stamp their ticket, tell them it was all right. He looked around the room to clear his head, grinding his teeth some more and sweating. "Well, I'll tell you . . ." he began, as if getting ready to go.

"Would you like to sit down?" Archie said. "Let me buy you a drink."

"Well . . ." Billy began, shifting uncomfortably on his feet, telling himself to just breathe, and that it would be over in a second. "I really ought to get over here and see my sister. I don't get home too often, and when I do, I like to visit as much as possible."

The encounter was not going according to the scenario Archie had envisioned. Still, he had to ask the question on his mind, out of pure curiosity. "Billy," Archie said, "can I ask you, how did you remember my name?"

Billy didn't fully understand the question; to him it seemed as if the man facing him was trying to make a point about his age. "Partner," Billy began, "I'm not as senile as I might look. Don't push me, now. I'm sorry I acted up, but I gotta go see my sister."

Archie sensed that if he was going to say what he had wanted to say, he would have to say it quickly. "Billy," he began, "I just wanted to tell you—"

"Jesus goddamn it," Billy said, leaning across the table toward his old schoolmate, his forehead dripping sweat and his eyes burning. "Don't say it. Stop right there. You love me, right?"

Archie was so taken aback by this outburst that he blurted out the word "Yes," hardly even knowing he was saying it.

But before Archie had formed the word Billy had already pushed himself away from the table, turned around and walked away, barely able to rein in his contempt for all those fools who wanted some kind of salvation from someone like him.

LOSING HAND

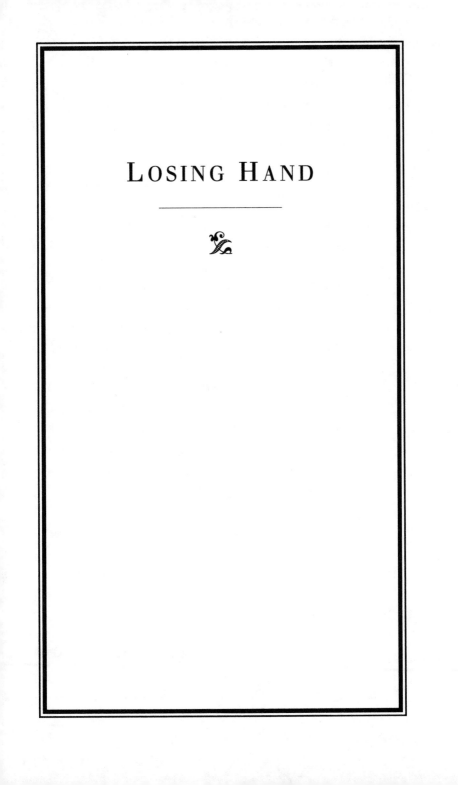

L ate. Down the beach the Santa Monica pier burns in the night. In the dark ocean off Malibu the tankers move heavily past each other. Downstairs, bare wet feet slap around the pool, with its stenciled depth numbers. In this suite, the garish flowered bamboo furniture sits like a group of gypsy women discussing me in a language I can't understand.

I'm so tired. You don't see the sun come up over the ocean here; you watch it go down over the ocean. It's like sitting facing backward on a train. This room will be here after time stops, after the last bomb is dropped, after the television runs out of reruns, when there is only one man left, lurching down the cracked, sun-baked mud banks of the river that runs along by Fornaci, perhaps wearing fatigues, in any case with a dazed and anguished expression on his face, maybe carrying a carbine, and coming upon the small shack, where the eggs are still warm, the butter melting on the toast, no MPs anywhere . . . dozing . . .

I have a flight out at eight-thirty in the morning; it will all get smaller behind me, Venice Beach, Rae's Diner, all of it running through my fingers like sand. Then shreds of cloud, gauze, sun getting stronger, the roller skaters invisible now, somebody next to me asking where I'm going . . . She might still call and repeal my sentence, save me from years of forced conversation with strangers.

Three nights ago she told me that she wasn't ready to leave Vic. Her voice was squeezed down by thousands of miles of telephone cable to essentials, to the thinnest of threads, from which I hung, desperate by then to hear even bad news. After we got off I felt myself disappearing into the night sky, hurtling backward into black space. I drove five hours, got into a bus and then onto a plane, flew all night and landed in L.A. like a paratrooper behind enemy lines.

We ate dinner in Paradise Cove. Vic was in Telluride for a few days. She looked beautiful. She phased in and out. She felt guilty. Then she'd forget it. Then it would come back. We sat in the candlelight, the ocean black outside the glass, which showed only our dark reflections, looking into each other's eyes. The situation was so dramatic that there wasn't much to talk about. After dinner, walking out in the parking lot with the ocean in the background, she felt good again. I carried her over my shoulder. We went back to the place she and Vic share in Santa Monica.

On the beach at North Truro this summer she told me about his breakdown, about her book contract, about how she got out to L.A. in the first place. Amazing, exhilarating confidences. Summer was ending. Notes were delivered. There were long silences listening to the tide coming in. We waded through knee-deep water, looking for the remains of Irish clay pipes from a boat that crashed a hundred years ago. We swam at midnight in the bioluminescent August bay, where every dive from the moored Sunfish was traced by electric green bubbles.

Her father's eyes are gray, like a wolf's; he stares at an invisible enemy in the middle distance, lost in an alcoholic trance. Her mother is on the boards of three museums. Her brother lives in a cardboard box outside Tucson and makes sculptures from beer cans. Jean survived, like a rose in a railroad yard, or an arrow from a dead man's bow. But she pays: leaves from hedges have to be folded three times across and once lengthwise. She purchases certain items only at certain stores. All the summer houses along the bay had family names associated with them, known since childhood, which she forced me to memorize. She applied lip balm regularly from a small jar, using her fourth finger and staring into the middle distance.

Moonlight, low tide; we took our shoes off next to the Surfside Inn and walked back the rest of the way along the beach. The whole shambling curve of lights of Provincetown lay off in the distance. Boats were stranded on the flats. The sand, deep down, was riddled with shells and buried crockery, clay pipe stems, broken pieces of porcelain dolls. There was an inevitability about it, anything sanctioned in that way by the moon. You are part of a tradition, of something larger.

The sunlight returns your outlines to you. She left for L.A. the next morning.

At their apartment in Santa Monica, I stood in the dark as she first turned on one muted table lamp, then another. There was a couch, a fireplace. The blue shadows, the implicit nearness of the sea, the conspiratorial closeness of the night, put us back in some zone we shared even before we met. We slept on a fold-out sofa; she didn't want to spend the night in their bed. Lying there in the dark, talking in her ear, hearing her in mine again, kissing and finally drifting to sleep along the curve of a hand . . .

In the morning I awoke to crisp door frames outlined in sunlight, framed posters, fireplace tongs in a basket. The ambush of another person's life was all around: pictures of them together lying in wait on a bureau, standing outside a hotel in Las Vegas, or on the beach in Cancun. How to compete with the mornings of grapefruit on the terrace, the intimacy of coming out of the shower while the other makes the bed. Over breakfast, she told me she had unfinished business with him. The evidence was all around: the accumulated fact of their experiences together, things collected together, flesh of experience knitting.

After breakfast she showed me the city as if it were an embarrassing secret she had been keeping. I leaned forward to see the palm trees of Beverly Hills as I drove. We received pamphlets on reincarnation with our lemonade at the La Brea Tar Pits. We bought the unbelievably lurid woven religious postcards of Olvera Street, and the sun came through the high windows and gloom of Union Station. The day was a version of happiness in microcosm, as fragile and unrealistic as a ship in a bottle. In the afternoon cigarette smoke haze of Philippe's I almost passed out on a counter and she brought me soup.

It was getting toward evening when she dropped me off. She was going to a premiere with her friend Marta and Marta's husband, a producer. It wasn't dark yet, but you could sense lights being turned on, work being put to bed for the night, cocktails being poured, faces being made up. She stayed in her car as I walked inside, after we kissed good-bye. She mouthed the words "I love you." I told her she could call me when she got home later, no matter what time it was. I went to dinner alone, then came back here. I've been waiting for her to call, to remember the moon outside the window, the tide creeping in, the electric green bubbles in the obsidian water, waiting for her to prove I'm not just a figment of her imagination, something she needed to shim up one end of a life where everything was sliding off the table.

I'm going to wait until the last moment to leave, until the sun comes up like a gangster over Mulholland Drive and the gypsy women have gone to sleep and I can see the writing on the wall. As I drive to the airport through the cool, shadowed streets, I will fade in her mind like a constellation in the morning sky. She'll wait until the plane takes off and the gauzy clouds waft past the windows like static gathering as a radio station fades, and then she'll emerge like a fugitive into the brilliant sunlight and run to the ocean to make a new start.

SLOWING DOWN

C ruising down 95 just south of Jacksonville; the sun is going down, and the breeze is whipping in the windows, and I'm trying to figure out what I'm doing. I was headed for Daytona Beach until a few minutes ago, when a familiar panic started filling my stomach, like neon, flashing the word *trap* in bright blue letters.

I've been on interstates for days, since I walked out on Wanda, with Key West as my destination. But when I hit Florida an hour back, I began to wonder what I was going to do in Key West. I'd get out of the car, look around, cross the street, look in a store window, cross the street again. Sooner or later I'd have to get back in the car and drive back up the same long causeway I'd driven down. I began to feel edgy just thinking about it.

So I decided I would go to Daytona Beach first, just as a place to grab a bite and consider my options. But now the miles are unwinding like a tape getting close to the end of the spool, and I'm realizing I'm not ready for Daytona, either. The idea of stepping out of the car at some destination and having to figure out what to do with myself is not sitting well. I feel like I need to slow down a little first and get used to the idea.

I know exactly what Wanda would say about this. "You can't keep running away from your problems," she yelled after me as I walked down the driveway three days ago. "You better sit still and look inside yourself."

That attitude is exactly what I came out here to get away from. I plan to run away from my problems for as long as I can afford gasoline.

I grab the atlas off the passenger seat and open it to Florida. I'm going about 75, and I have to switch my glance back and forth between the road and the map. There's an exit for a red line called 207, which would take me out of my way, toward someplace called Palatka, then I could pick up 100 around San Mateo and head back and either get on 1 into Daytona or get back on 95 and keep going. The map is proof that I still have choices. The exit for 207 is, in fact, coming up on the right.

I swerve across two lanes and hit the ramp too quickly, but I apply the brakes in a series of short shots as I descend, slow, slower, and ease into a nice, gentle stop at the bottom of the ramp, at a traffic light.

A car whizzes by on the interstate above.

Across the intersection is an abandoned clapboard house, with a porch that has collapsed in the middle. No people around at all. The breeze has stopped whipping in, and it's very hot. The light changes and I make a left under the interstate bridge.

I'm on a two-lane blacktop road that crumbles at the edges where it meets the grass on either side. Trailer homes, cars up on cinderblocks. The late shadows cut across the grass and marshy dirt. For days, whole undigested conversations with Wanda have played themselves over in my mind like insomniac reruns at three in the morning. She told me I didn't know how to compromise. Arguments happened as if neither of us had any say in them. Everything was beginning to seem plotted out in advance. I could feel life slipping away. I couldn't stand it anymore, so I thought I'd hit the road and see something new.

Right now, I'm seeing small houses every quarter of a mile, rusted-out pickup trucks, refrigerators lying on their sides. A lone tree here and there in the distance or by the roadside, but mainly scrub. The whole area smacks of pensions, reading glasses, bad reception on television sets, old men in corduroy pants farting and arguing with their wives about something that happened forty years ago.

Wanda used to say, "Why do you have so much trouble just doing the simple things? That's what life is all about."

And I used to tell her I hated doing the laundry and washing dishes and putting up shelves, and she'd say, "Well, what do you want to do?" It used to make me crazy, because there's no answer to that question. You know, if I knew what I wanted to do, I'd be doing it. And if I'm not doing it, maybe I don't really want to do it. So I told her that, and she just sat there with this frown she gets between her eyes, just like a crease there that makes me want to put my fist through a wall.

A faint, high-pitched whistle pulls me out of my reverie. I've gone about ten miles on this blacktop road, and there are no houses around at all. The Pontiac is missing beats, and it lurches, misses, picks up and lurches forward, skips again, and the whining has gotten louder, and there's steam coming out from under the hood. I pull off onto the grass at the side of the road, and now there's lots of steam coming out and the engine's knocking and I cut the motor, with the engine knocking a few more times and clouds of steam surrounding the car.

Silence. Except for the sound of steam escaping, it's very quiet. This is more or less the worst thing that could be happening right now. I open the door, step out, and let the door close by itself. The ground is moist and spongy. I walk around and open the hood to give the engine some air. There couldn't be less breeze if this were the bottom of the Sargasso Sea. The sun has gone down, but it's still light. Little clouds of gnats hover at eye level above the blacktop. Three geese fly across the sky in slow motion, as if they're flying through motor oil. I get back into the Pontiac and sit behind the wheel. I rest my arm on the window ledge. This isn't my landscape. As far as I'm concerned, I'm still moving through it.

After a while, in the distance, I can see some kind of vehicle coming toward me. I step out into the middle of the road and wave my arm, pointing to the Pontiac. The car slows as it approaches, pulling slightly to the side as it stops.

The old man who's driving has rolled down his window, but he doesn't look up at me. He's got a crew cut, reddish, tough-looking skin, and an open-neck plaid flannel shirt with a T-shirt on underneath. He just keeps looking down the road.

"Engine trouble?" he says.

"I guess," I say.

"Well," he says, "I haven't got any jumper cables." He gets a private smile on his face and leans over to stub out his cigarette in the ashtray. It's a beat-up old car, some relic of the last paycheck the old bastard probably ever saw. Threadbare upholstery, not much inside except some rags on the shelf by the rear window, and a plastic trash bag, tied up at the top, which takes up half the backseat. "Hop in and I'll drive you to Leo's if you want."

"That's . . . a service station?" I ask.

"That's right," he says, looking straight out the front windshield of his car.

I look back across the road at my poor old Pontiac. I really don't have a choice. I go around the car and climb in, and he takes off almost before the door shuts, heading back in the direction I just came from. Leo's must be all the way on the other side of the interstate; I didn't see anything between there and where the car stopped.

The old guy's eyes are fixed straight ahead and he isn't saying anything. Despite the ripped upholstery, the car is clean inside, no dirt or paper on the floor. There's a small tattoo on his forearm; sure—he was in the service somewhere. Everybody his age was in the service. Probably retired, down here squeezing out the last few years.

The interstate overpass looms, then passes over us, and we come out on the other side. The old guy is tooling along pretty good. Still plenty of spirit; probably used to be a pilot or something. Narrow cockpits with real leather in those days, kept the cockpit clean too, had to; weekend nights in the bars, maybe in New Mexico; was he married yet? I feel myself cranking up, but I'm nipping it in the bud. I'm not going to be part of his plot, or vice versa. No plots, Jack. Just get me to Leo's. Get me to Daytona.

We've gone about five miles past the interstate and we're cranking along, the old guy is staring out the front window, and it's beginning to feel a little funny to me. It's not natural to say nothing at all to someone you've picked up. Not even "Come a ways?" or "Where you headin'?" Maybe he's just quiet. We're getting pretty far away from the Pontiac. We passed a small convenience store about two miles back with a couple gas pumps out front, but now we're out in the flats again. It's taking too long, so I say, "How much farther is Leo's?"

He keeps looking out the front window, shrugs his shoulders. I'm waiting for something else, but that's it. After a minute he fishes a pack of cigarettes out of his breast pocket, gives it a shake and holds it out to me with two cigarettes sticking up.

"No thanks," I say. He pulls one out with his lips, puts the pack back in his pocket and pushes in the lighter. Maybe he didn't hear me. "Leo's coming up soon?" I say.

He pulls out the lighter and lights his cigarette, replaces

the lighter. We're going through empty marsh country, like the kind the Pontiac is still in. Nothing but marsh around, out to the horizon, one or two trailer homes . . .

"I just shot my wife," he says.

The hair on my arms is standing up. I look over at him; he seems lost in thought. There's no way of knowing if it's true or not. There's a chance I only imagined he said it. It's probably obvious that I'm not responding, but what should I say—"When?" "What was her name?" "How long were you married?"

The trailers seem to be nebulizing; we might be coming to a town, but it's hard to tell. I'm thinking I'll ask him to drop me off as soon as there are some other people around. The hell with Leo's, if it even exists.

"Did you ever eat a chicken that you'd killed yourself?" he says.

I actually think about this for a second, although the answer couldn't be more accessible to me.

"No," I say.

He's chuckling a little, as if he's in on some secret of mine, as if he's finally got my number. "Is it still on the stove?" he asks me. We are indeed coming to something like a town here; the trailers are more densely concentrated than they have been, and we in fact pass a gas station and don't stop.

"Uh, listen," I say, "you know what . . . I'll hop out here maybe, okay?" The car is speeding up.

He doesn't say anything now as we drive out the other end of town, past another convenience store, into the deepening plum blue of the evening, and I realize I've got to ditch. I pull on the door latch, even as I feel him speeding up some more, and try to push the door open against the force of the air pushing back. With a lunge of energy I wedge myself into a parachutist's position, get the door open enough and the next thing is my feet going out from under me . . .

I'm with a face against the black asphalt in the night air I think. It is definitely warm against my arms. I look up, across; taillights down the road squeeze brighter for a second, then fade away. I roll onto my back. It's night, all right. The stars are very close down, here in the open. I lie still for a moment, feeling the heat from the blacktop seeping up through me.

I stand and get out of the road. My knee hurts, but I can walk. I head for a diner in a parking lot maybe a hundred yards away. The first thing I want is a phone. It's a real old-fashioned diner from the outside, a lot like the one I used to pass on the Taconic Parkway when I was in school. That was where Sheehan got sick the night we went to the concert in Schenectady. Except Schenectady was in the other direction. The hell with the sheets. Something about a candle. They had delicious cheesecake. Fluorescent light spills out the window, only three cars in the parking lot, kind of an old railroad-car style.

The diner is empty, except for a waitress down at the end of the counter to the left, smoking a cigarette and talking on a phone attached to the wall. She doesn't look up. I look around to see if there's a pay phone. Another waitress backs out through the twin swinging steel doors from the kitchen, carrying a giant silverware tray.

I start to ask her about the phone, but she cuts me off, says, "Not now," and walks down the counter away from me with the tray, which she can barely handle. The other one is just looking down at her elbow and letting the smoke curl up to the ceiling, listening to the phone.

This is what *The Twilight Zone* must have been like during a commercial. I look around in the entryway a little more, then I hear a sickening crash from the far end of the diner, and the second waitress screaming, "Son of a bitch! Son of a bitch!" The first waitress glances toward her, then looks at me and rolls her eyes as if to say, "I put up with this all the time."

I can hear the other one sobbing, scrabbling around, trying to pick up the silverware. I can't just stand here; I head down to see if I can give her a hand.

She's on her knees, grabbing forks. I say, "Hey, can I—" but she cuts me off and says, "Can I get this cleaned up first?"

I say, "I was going to help you."

"Oh," she says, "I'm sorry. You can help me."

I kneel and start gathering spoons and forks.

"If she got paid for making phone calls, she'd be a millionaire by now," she says. "Talk and smoke, talk and smoke, like the burning bush."

"I was hoping I could make a call myself," I say.

"I wouldn't bet any money on it."

"Is there a pay phone anywhere?"

"They took it out," she says. "People were abusing the privilege."

We get the last of it picked up and set on the counter. I say, "Listen, I've got to make a call. My car broke down."

She looks at me as if for the first time. "You're all banged up."

"I had to jump out of a car."

She frowns, so I say, "I had to hitchhike here because my car broke down."

"Why'd you come here for? You need a garage if your car broke down." She's frowning a little more, so I breathe deeply and tell her about the old guy.

"I would never hitchhike around here; people are crazy," she says. "They found one guy in the marshes dressed up like a gorilla with his head split open. It was after Halloween."

I don't want to know about this. I tell her I didn't have much choice because of my car breaking down, and what I need is to tell the police and to get a garage for the car.

"Are you sure you don't need a doctor?" she says. "I don't know what we'd do in here if there was an emergency. We probably wouldn't even be able to get a call to let us know if the Russians had landed." She says this loud enough for the other one to hear.

From down the counter, the other one covers her mouthpiece and says, "What is your problem? Why don't you just go find yourself a boyfriend and stop harassing me?"

"This man just jumped out of a car and he needs a doctor and he could bleed to death on the floor by the time you get finished."

The waitress at the far end says a few things into the phone and then hangs up. The one I was with says, "Hold on; I'll call up the hospital."

"Wait a second," I say. "I don't need the hospital. I need a garage. . . ."

"Stay there; I'll call." She runs to the far end, past the other waitress, and picks up the phone. The waitress who had been on the phone comes down to me.

"Are you okay?" she says. "She's nuts. Don't worry about her."

"I'm more or less fine," I say. This waitress is good-looking, sexy, and she is leaning across the counter toward me, giving me a good look down her blouse. She's wearing bright red lipstick. The other one is jabbering away and I'm trying to hear what she's saying. "I don't need a doctor," I say. "I need to get to Daytona Beach. I hope she's not calling the hospital."

"I told you, she's nuts. What're you going to Daytona for?"

"Uh . . . I've got business there," I say. I don't even know what I'm saying. I'm trying to hear the other waitress. She's looking nervously toward us.

"Shit, I'll drive you to Daytona. Let me tell nutso down here."

She runs down behind the counter, and I'm thinking, Maybe this is what I want. Maybe I should just get to Daytona and worry about the Pontiac later. Maybe all this is exactly what I need on some level.

I hear raised voices again. The one who dropped the silverware is saying, "What am I supposed to do while you're driving all over the place? Grow two more arms? Forget it."

"You forget it. I'll be back in a couple hours, if I come back." She grabs a giant yellow purse from next to the milk shake machine and starts back around the counter.

The one with the silverware is crying again. A guy in his forties has just walked in, wearing a flannel shirt and a mesh cap that says Smith & Wesson on it. He sits down and looks over at them.

"Go on ahead and cry; you got customers." She grabs her coat off a hook, digs some keys out of her purse and says, "Come on, let's get out of here before we go crazy, too."

I'm watching this, not knowing what to do. I didn't cause this problem; all I want is to get to Daytona at this point. I can call a garage from there. The new guy is reading a menu; he doesn't want to know about anything, either. I follow the smoker out the door.

It's dark outside under the Florida sky. She walks with a quick step, shaking her head and jingling her car keys, toward a car in the shadows to the left of the entrance. I catch up with her as she opens the door, and I run around to the passenger side and slide in.

"Thank God we're out of there," she says. "You'd think she was one of the biggest saints who ever lived. I don't know what she was telling you, but let me tell you, it probably was a gigantic exaggeration. She's one of these people who think their problems are the most interesting thing that ever happened on the face of the earth."

I don't really want to hear this, but she's throwing off some kind of animal attraction that is getting to me. I'm starting to plot; it would be so easy to say a few of the right things and get a room for fifteen bucks in a hotel down the road somewhere, the only light in the room a frosted over-head fixture with dead mosquitoes in the bottom. But it would go against the whole spirit of this trip. I don't want to muddy the stream; I want to stick to my plan—drive, watch, no surprises, me in control, peace, harmony, no un-seen ramifications . . .

"Like, she says I don't do enough work in there. If she spent as much energy working as she does complaining, that place would be more popular than McDonald's. Then her latest little song and dance is that I talk too much on the phone. If you noticed, most of what I do is listen. I think we're put in this world to help other people for the most part, like if somebody needs a ride to Daytona, you give it to them, and you don't make a big fuss over having to do a lit-tle extra work."

She sticks her key into the ignition and turns it and the car zooms to life. In one motion, she slides it into reverse and steps on the gas and we shoot backward and there's a horrible lurch and loud sound of crunching metal and show-ering glass and we stop, jerking backward and then forward.

"God damn shit," she says, opening the door and jump-ing out, slamming it behind her. I hear her walking around outside the car. A second later the diner door opens and the guy in the flannel shirt comes out. We backed square into the side of a pickup truck. He comes walking quickly over, yelling out, "Jesus! Jesus! What the goddamn hell happened?"

"What does it look like happened? Your goddamn truck was parked right in back of me."

"What are you, blind? Look at this. . . ."

"Look at me; I'm busted up all over the place."

"I'm gonna have to get a whole new door."

"Well, what do you call this? I got no taillights."

"The hell with your taillights. How am I supposed to get into my truck?"

"The hell with you, homo head. Why'd you have to park right there for? Isn't the parking lot big enough?"

"Watch your dirty mouth. . . ."

I'm sitting here listening to this, thinking, What's it gonna take? What do I have to do? Why did I get off the interstate? These people were probably all happy until I got here. I hear her voice rise; it sounds like a scuffle. Yep—"Get your hands off me. . . ."

I open the door and step out and I see her banging on his head with her hands, and he's trying to grab her around the neck. "Hey," I say, coming around the car, "that's all. That's all," I say as I try to pry his arms off her. "Hey."

They're really going at it, so I have to reach in to stop things, and I finally break his hold and push him off and he trips backward and falls on his ass looking up at me, and he's on his feet in a second before I can say anything, charging me like a bull, and I don't want to, but I feint down to the right and come up and across with a picture book right cross and his legs go—I can see them wave—and he falls back and knocks his head against her car bumper and lands, out cold. He's really out.

"Shit, you killed him," she says, taking a step back.

"Stop it," I say, bending over the guy. She's starting to really get on my nerves now. He's got an ugly gash over his ear, some blood, but not deep, just nasty. His jaw's a little swollen, too. I need this like I need hepatitis. He'll be okay. The cut could take a couple stitches, probably.

I tell her to grab his ankles, and I grab him under the arms. We lift him; he's heavy. Up the stairs and back inside, and we lay him on the counter.

"Jesus God," the first waitress screams. "Why'd you do that?"

"He hit him 'cause he was trying to beat me up," my friend says.

"I'm gonna call the police ambulance," the first one says.

"Wait a second," I say. "Let's put some water on this cut and see how he is."

"I knew there was something wrong with you," the first one says, taking a step backward.

"Look out for the coffee maker," my waitress says, but she spoke too late, and the first one trips and falls backward, bumping her head on the swinging doors, howling in pain.

"We're never going to hear the end of this," my friend says.

---

* * *

It's two-thirty in the morning. I'm in a fluorescent yellow emergency room, sitting on a bench. Lesley, the waitress, has been in the ladies' room for fifteen minutes. This place is way too bright. The only other person waiting is an old man in a T-shirt who looks like he's been asleep since Garibaldi conquered the Mennonites. Flies buzz around the curtained-off beds, and the orderly in charge is watching *The Love Boat* on a miniature television behind the desk. I'm almost beginning to wish I had never come to Florida. I am staying awake because I have accepted the chlorinated linoleum, the disinfectant-flavored ashtrays, the chicken wire holding everybody's skulls together . . .

"Hey, wake up."

I shake my head; Lesley is sitting down next to me. "Scoot over a little. You got drool on your chin."

I scuff it off with my wrist and slide over to make room. "How long was I asleep?"

"How do I know? I just came back in."

"What time is it?"

"It's three million o'clock."

"Is the detective still around?"

"I haven't seen him if he is. Jesus, what a bad complexion he's got."

I rub my eyes. My brain feels like a side of corned beef on a steam table in an Irish bar. Alligators have probably already dragged the seats out of my car; I didn't even think to lock it. I'm trying to remember why all this happened in the first place. I should have gone straight through to Daytona. You can't slow down if you're skating on thin ice. I could leave this emergency room anytime, I guess, but there's no place to go. I'll probably just sleep on this bench and then consider my options when it gets light outside.

She's putting on lipstick, looking at herself in a pocket mirror. "You know," she says, as if she read my mind, "if you want to stay at my house tonight, you can." She presses her lips together, checking them in the mirror. "You can sleep in the den. My ex-husband has the downstairs apartment, but he sleeps late, so there shouldn't be any confusion."

"Your ex-husband?" I say. It's getting so I can smell out a bad situation from miles away.

"We're friends. I told him he had to move out, and there was an apartment open downstairs, like a finished basement? We stay out of each other's hair for the most part."

"How's he going to feel about my being there?"

"Well, he made his decision. I don't care what he does, and he knows what's gonna happen if he starts any shit."

Through the electric yellow gloom I can see it all in advance. The husband will come in drunk at four in the morning to borrow a can opener. The drawer will stick from the dampness, and he'll go crazy and throw a chair through the window. Lesley will wake up and pull a gun on him; he'll turn out the lights and there will be a struggle. I'll see the flash of the gun going off twice. Suddenly, with a noise like a plane taking off, an elephant's head will burst through the wall, and the house will collapse like a cardboard building in a Japanese science-fiction movie as P. T. Barnum him-self leads his entire troupe through on the way to Disney World. They will be followed, as they always are, by killer ants, then flamingos, then newspaper reporters. . . .

"What's the matter?" she says, looking at me.

"Nothing," I say. She has a panicked look on her face.

"Look," she says, "I know I come on strong. I scare men away sometimes. I know that. Am I doing that now?"

I'm startled by the fear in her eyes, and I scramble around in my head, trying to think of something appropriate to say to avoid having to deal with this. She dabs at her eyes with a tissue that she has taken from her giant yellow purse and, before I can think of what to say, the purse tumbles from her leg and dumps, upside down, on the floor. We stare down at it for a moment, as if we've witnessed a car crash from a helicopter, then I jump onto my hands and knees and start gathering the stuff, thanking God for this diversion.

I right the purse so I can put things into it—a packet of tissues, two tampons, a felt-tip pen with no cap, a swizzle stick that says *Hilltop Lounge*—I didn't know they had hills in Florida. . . . As soon as I get this stuff picked up, I'm going to call a taxi and go to Daytona if it costs me a hun-dred dollars. I'm just going to get a room in Daytona and lock the door. A picture ID driver's license; she had her hair different. You can tell a lot about somebody from this kind of stuff. If you could assemble enough of these things, the evidence of all these choices, they might fill in a picture of who somebody is, like the dots in a newspaper photograph.

A small crossword puzzle book, a bunch of color samples

on a plastic ring, a plastic rose, three Mexican coins, a small card with bobby pins on it. Let's say the color samples are for the walls she's repainting in the kitchen. The Mexican coins must be from a vacation, a splurge with a girlfriend, or maybe some guy. Maybe that's where the rose is from, too. Sitting out on a deck sipping piña coladas and imagining some romantic future for herself, exotic lizards combing the sand as the sun sinks into a lagoon and hula dancers tell the story of the great bird that created the world. I wonder what someone would think if my pockets dumped on the floor. Car keys, maps, money . . . what else? What could you tell about me from my things? I get restless when there are too many things around. As I think this, the image of the old man who picked me up earlier flashes into my mind, and suddenly I picture myself like that—old, alone, driving around with a bag of secrets in my backseat. . . .

"Let me help," Lesley says, and she's kneeling next to me, with a little pink plastic bow barrette in her hair. "All this stuff I collect," she says, shaking her head.

I can feel myself losing it, dissolving like a sugar cube in a sloe gin fizz. I've made no contact with anybody for days, and I think it's catching up with me. I must have chosen this on some level, but it doesn't feel like I've chosen it. All I've been thinking about is what I don't want. I don't want to wash the dishes or build shelves. I don't want to go to Key West. I don't want to get stuck with someone who will ask me a lot of questions, or tell me their story. But what do I want? That's what Wanda used to ask me all the time. Why am I spending all this energy just so I don't have to answer that question? I'm getting this creepy feeling like maybe I'm not even really alive. But she's alive—I can see she has this whole life that I don't even have a clue about.

"Listen," I blurt out, before I even think about it. "I'll stay at your place tonight. But can you do something?"

"What?" she says, suspiciously.

"Tell me . . ." I begin, ". . . about where you grew up."

"I grew up in Tallahassee," she says. "That's about the most boring story you'd ever hear."

"I want to hear it," I say.

She's frowning a little, but she shrugs and says, "All right. It's your funeral."

But what if there's nothing to talk about in the morning, and it's raining outside? What if she has a white-painted bedroom set and stuffed animals? What if, what if, what if . . . I take a slow, deep breath, then let it out as slowly as I can. I'm staring down at something that has just come into focus. It's a small, fake wood-grained plaque like you'd buy in a five-and-ten, with a picture of two lion cubs on it, and some lettering reading "Friends are life's sunshine." The lamination has bubbled up in one corner.

"My mama gave me that," she says.

"It's real cute," I say. Relax, I tell myself. Relax and take what comes. After a moment she pulls out a pack of chewing gum and holds the pack out to me.

"Gum?" she says.

"Yes," I say. "Good. Thanks," and I take a piece, hoping that maybe I'm taking a small step in the right direction.

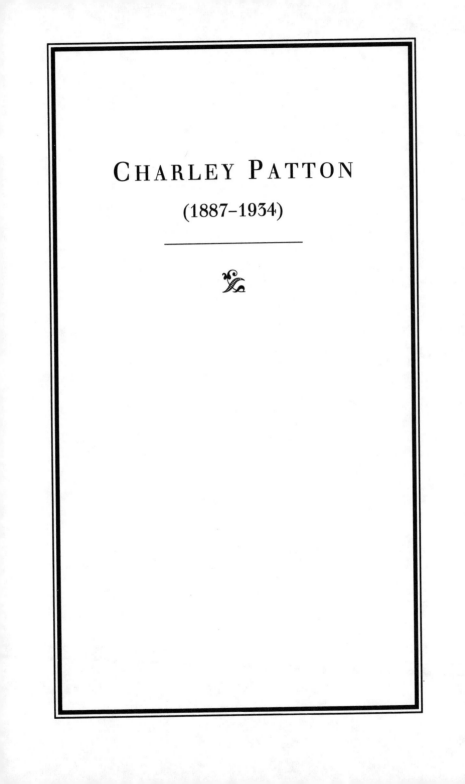

CHARLEY PATTON

(1887–1934)

The unseen wraps itself in the visible facts, the curbs that crumble in the midday sun, the street you follow out of town, the dirt road, the tin awning, the fireplace empty in the empty house, the fields almost brown in the haze, the scraps of old wallpaper, brown with the years, the woodsmoke in the tree branches and your grandfather invisible in the darkening blue evening, searching for fireflies.

The southbound train, the crossing in the gray afternoon, the bookstore in the town square; the farmhouse seen from the speeding car, the maps tucked in the glove compartment, the warm food in the brown paper bag, the rough wool blanket in the houndstooth plaid, the minutes spent waiting in the chill passenger seat under the stars.

In the kitchen the women baste the roasting meat; the husbands have gone to the bakery for warm rolls. Downstairs, the parade flickers on the television in the empty den. The children walk up the sidewalk in the sharp midmorning air through the crisp leaves to the old brick school on the hill, closed for vacation, the small-paned windows reflecting the cloudless blue sky, and the varnished wood floors inside quiet in the dark halls.

And the sunlight on the car bumper, the sparrow pecking in the shade near the curb, the tricycle in the tall grass, it sits there still, waiting for the highway to come through, or the afternoon mail, or the five o'clock whistle, the dinner bell—a single frame, on pause, under great tension, drops of condensation forming as the great eye circles the earth, measures it yet again . . .

The choruses could go on forever, it seems, like counties, heading west, or railroad ties, the limitless vistas, the herds of buffalo, the inexhaustible mornings, and all the while, time, like a snake eating away at the egg, slithering back to collect its due, the assassin's mark, not quite dead, climbing back from the ravine with a knife in its teeth.

And this brittle shellac disc, like a black full moon, its grooves a long thin scar spiraling imperceptibly toward the center, the inevitable ending, awash in the crumbling hiss and crackle of time's bonfire, but always to begin again, if someone will place the needle once more at the outer rim, to hear the hiss, the crackle, the imperceptibly high guitar notes and then the voice, flaring up and dying down like a kitchen match, singing again of all the old familiar places,

The long, deserted street, the sun hot on the brick sidewalk, the shadows under the balconies, the dusty wine-colored hotel drapes, the red light flashing on the portable recorder, the long moment of free-fall, and then the high guitar notes, again . . .

The morning train, damp and blue-gray in the haze, the grasshoppers jumping on the dirt road to the crossing, the billows of steam in the morning air, the haze burning off, the spools of telegraph wire, the gravel by the depot still wet in the morning dew, the tracks disappearing around the curve like a snake in the weeds, heading north toward Chicago and history,

All but forgotten now, the endless schedules and revisions of schedules, the timetables, the porter's voice amid the sleeping figures curled in the seats in deep midnight, the small towns along the way, where one or two will step down heavily and still full of sleep onto the station platform and back into the world . . .

So long the afternoon's broad shadows when they finish for the day; the red light clicks off and the drapes open and he counts his money, and outside the shadows creep up the brick storefronts as the street submerges toward evening and steak and whiskey and yet another room somewhere, and the wax masters are packed carefully and sent, things now, only, still fluid, still destructible, but hardening, toward the pressing plant.

Burn another year, and another, a leaping tiger circling the track, the girls jumping rope under the banana trees, and all the while waiting in the back of the store on West Main in the broad afternoon amid the oak chairs, broken bedstands, lamps and fixtures, the stacks of them, forgotten now, left in frozen attitudes, awaiting the needle in the outer groove, the hiss and crackle, the always beginning again, which is not remembering but something else—

The cloud shadows moving on the hillside, the shivering leaves in the sudden breeze, the woodstove in the empty depot, the blues like showers of rain.